To/ MY LOVELY FRIEND
KAREN

SAVIOUR

OF THE

SOUL

C.L. Stewart

SAVIOUR OF THE SOUL

Copyright © 2019 Paper Chain Publishing

All rights reserved. This book or any portion thereof may not be reproduced or used in any manner whatsoever without the express written permission of the publisher except for the use of brief quotations in a book review.

First published 2016
Second edition 2019

www.clstewart.co.uk

ISBN: 9781999319328

For Mary, My Fabulous Mum.

You made me the person I am, and I will be forever thankful to you. I love you to the moon and back. xx

ACKNOWLEDGMENTS

My thanks have to go to all my readers who took a chance and read Shattered Soul. Gina and Steven will always have a special place in my heart and it makes me happy to know that their story has been taken to your hearts too.

PROLOGUE

THE YELLOWING PAINTED BRICK walls of the prison cell comfort him. Prison is basically his home. Really who wouldn't like it? Three meals a day, TV in his cell and, most of the time, a decent cell mate.

He likes routine. Routine helps him with his plans. Okay getting jailed again wasn't part of the plan. He was stupid to think Cheryl wouldn't do something when she found out he had been released. He hadn't counted on her getting friendly with Steven though. Why would he? She hated Steven almost as much as he did.

Best to bide his time and play nice. There's always somebody willing to do things on the outside for the right price and when he eventually gets out, he will make them pay. All of them, and they won't know what's hit them.

CHAPTER 1

WHENEVER I THINK OF Christmas I am reminded of my childhood, when the festive season started as soon as it hit the first of December. Mum would pester dad to get the tree and decorations down from the attic so that we could festoon the house. We always started with the lights. Testing them to make sure they still worked. In the days before LED lights if one bulb was out the whole string didn't work. Many a first of December was spent pulling and replacing every bulb to find out which one had blown. Inevitably it would always be the last one, no matter which end you started at.

Our house always ended up looking like a scene from Elf. Even when she was finished, she wasn't really finished. Every time she would go shopping or come home from work, she would have 'just one more thing' to add to Santa's Grotto. Dad eventually gave up, just smiled and let her get on with it.

My childhood Christmases were very happy. My childhood was very happy full stop, so you can imagine my shock at Steven's reaction when I mentioned putting up a Christmas tree in his apartment earlier this morning.

***

"Do you have a tree and decorations? This place needs some festivity. It's only a week till Christmas."

"I don't do Christmas," Steven declared with his back to me reading some papers.

"You don't do Christmas?"

"No.".

"Who on earth doesn't do Christmas? It's such a fun time of the year."

He shook his head and I could see his fists clench. "For fuck sake Gina leave it."

"I don't think there was any call for that Steven. I was only asking."

He turned to look at me, his expression solemn and angry. "Think about it Gina. I mean really think about what you are saying here before you go any further."

Light bulb.

"Tell me Gina, would you celebrate Christmas if every single one you had as a child was only another day? If every Christmas, you saw kids out on their new bikes or in their new clothes. If so many fucking Christmas dinners were a tin of beans or whatever you could find that wasn't out of date." He closed his eyes and shook his head. "If every fucking day you lived in... Oh, forget it Gina."

"I'm sorry Steven, I didn't think."

"No that's the problem when you've never had to deal with that sort of thing Gina. You think everyone lived in the same wee bubble you did." He lifted his papers and walked to the kitchen door.

"Where are you going? I said I was sorry."

"I have work to do." And with that he walked away leaving me sitting alone in the kitchen. God that was harsh. I heard him go upstairs and then a door slammed. Thank God, I had a horrible feeling he was going to walk out.

***

It's a little after three in the afternoon and the natural light is already fading. I haven't seen Steven since he went up to his office about four hours ago. I grab my phone and take the stairs as quietly as I can. I head into his walk-in wardrobe and gather up the Sexy Santa outfit he gave me. I really hope he sees the funny side of this, and I don't look like a complete fool. I forego the boots this time, they make too much noise, and

10

after plugging my iPhone into the dock in the bedroom I select the Christmas playlist. If this doesn't get me back in the good books, I don't know what will.

As the first strains of *'Santa Baby'* fill the speakers I tentatively open the office door. Steven's desk sits to the left of it facing the window. Hiding behind the door I stick my left leg out so that he can see it in all its candy cane glory. I put my hands down to my ankle and pull them up slowly. As the singing starts, I step into the room and see that Steven keeps his head down pretending he doesn't see me. I start my seductive little routine. I probably look ridiculous, but I really don't care. Standing with my back to him I gyrate my hips and stick out my bum and when I catch a glimpse of the now darkened window pane in front of me, I see that he is looking at me. And he is smiling. 'Yes! Victory'.

I make my way over to him, grab the arms of the chair and pull it far enough away from the desk so that I can straddle his lap.

The song finishes and Frank Sinatra comes crooning through the speakers. He looks into my eyes and smiles.

"What are you doing Gina?"

"Oh nothing."

"Does that feel like nothing?" He says as he pulls me closer to him, I can feel his erection through his

11

jeans.

"Mmm, absolutely not."

He puts his hands behind my head and pulls my lips to his. Our kiss is slow and sweet and seems to last forever. "I'm sorry Gina," Steven whispers against my lips as I lean back to look at him.

"Forget about it, I have. I get it Steven. I'm an idiot. I have this sort of malfunction; you know that brain to mouth thing. Sorry honey but it's just another one of those things you're going to have to love me for." I cock my head to the side and give him a little smile and a flutter of my eyelids. He throws his head back and laughs, a real hearty laugh that vibrates through me. His hands run down my back over the velour of the dress and come to rest on my backside.

"Gina, I am loving every little thing I am finding out about you." He looks down and gives a little shake of his head. "This isn't going to be easy is it?" He looks up at me and I can see the torment behind his eyes.

"No, it's not but you know something, look at what we've been through already. I have a feeling we'll be fine." I try my best to reassure him, but my own doubts start to creep in. When you have had your world pulled from under you it is hard to believe in anything

Steven kisses the top of my arm. "Want to go out for dinner?"

His ability to U-turn a subject frustrates me at times

but right now it's a welcome relief. As much as we need to talk about things that have gone on in our own lives, what happened to me is still raw, the wounds still too fresh.

"Sounds good to me. Shall we toss for it?"

"That sounds like heaven to me babe, but we might never make it to dinner if I let you do that." He throws me a sexy wink laughing at his own joke.

I swat him on the chest. "Oh, you insatiable beast."

As I stand up and turn away from him, he smacks my bum. "What can I do when you are dressed like that? I'm at your mercy woman."

"Right since your mind is firmly in the gutter, I'm choosing the cuisine. We'll do Italian tonight. I'm off to get dressed."

"You could go like that, I wouldn't mind."

I smile and pick up a cushion from the sofa in front of the window. "Beast," I laugh as I throw it at him. Then I bolt like a bat out of hell before he catches up with me.

CHAPTER 2

"GINA, GERRY IS HERE. Are you ready?" He shouts up the stairs.

Gerry has been summoned to pick us up and the Bentley is sitting at the kerb outside.

I am still trying to get ready. Steven had the car here within fifteen minutes of me suggesting an Italian for dinner.

I open the bedroom door and shout back. "Good God man do you realise how long it takes a lady to get ready. I still have to get dressed."

"Hurry up darling time is money." I can hear the smile in his voice.

I choose a pair of plain black trousers and an off-white sleeveless shell top and black jacket. It looks smart enough for dinner but not too dressed up. Steven took me shopping a few days ago and I now have a well-stocked wardrobe in one of his spare rooms. I've also had my hair lightened slightly and re-styled. I'm a newer happier version of me. I settle on a pair of silver sparkly sandals and, with a quick check of my appearance in the mirror on the landing, I head downstairs.

Steven is standing next to the piano with his back to me fiddling on his phone and turns when he hears me. "Very nice," he says and moves towards me as I stand on the second last step. He lifts me in his arms and kisses me as I slide down him to stand on the floor. He twirls my soft curls in his fingers. "I like this."

"Not so bad yourself handsome."

He looks casually yummy in his silvery grey dress trousers and white shirt with the sleeves rolled to slightly below the elbows. God his forearms should be illegal.

"Let's go before I tell Gerry to go and get us a take away instead." He winks at me and pulls me towards the door.

"Okay Mr Insatiable. Watch it…you may wear me out."

"That's my plan babe," he laughs.

Gerry is waiting outside and opens the door as soon as he sees us.

"Evening folks," he says and nods. "Looking lovely Gina as always."

"Thanks Gerry, as do you." I flash him a smile and look at Steven who is giving Gerry the evil eye.

"Sorry sir, you look good too," says Gerry with a smile. Ooh he's brave.

"You're a funny man Gerry. It's a good thing I like you." They both shake hands and I see the affection Steven has for Gerry in the look he gives the man. It's nice to see.

I get into the back of the car and Steven joins me. He places his hand on my thigh as Gerry closes the door. It's nice, but I am still very wary of every little thing that feels too good to be true.

A little over a week ago I got the shock of my life when I found out that my dead husband had been having an affair which had produced a child. And in a seriously messed up twist of fate I ended up having to help the girl deliver the baby after she ambushed me in my own home. It is constantly in the back of my mind that the one person I thought was the love of my life betrayed me. He was the one person I thought would always protect me.

I thought we were happy. It turns out I was the stupid sap who wanted to believe that there was good in everyone. Boy, how wrong was I? It made me realise that nothing in this life is certain or sure, that there are always going to be obstacles to overcome.

It is much harder to be happy than it is to be

miserable. Being miserable is easy you only need to shut yourself down. I know, I did it. Making yourself happy, no scratch that, allowing yourself to be happy takes hard work, time and plenty of soul searching. It also needs trust. That's what I know I am going to have the most trouble with. I know not everyone is the same; I know Steven is nothing like Aiden. In the four weeks or so I have known him he has managed to capture my heart. He has made me feel alive again and has done nothing but make me feel loved and safe. He has promised me he will never let me down.

I want so badly to believe him. I know I believe him on some level, but it will take time to get over what has happened. I can only hope his will is strong enough to hang around.

As the car pulls to a stop, I notice we are in a little side street off High Street in the city centre. This does not look like the sort of place a millionaire businessman takes his girlfriend to dinner. Yes, girlfriend, I have finally accepted that accolade, much to my best friend Charlie's relief.

Steven leans in to me and kisses my hair. "We're here babe. You hungry?"

"Yes, but where is here?"

"Ah, it's a surprise."

"Yay I just love surprises." Sarcasm drips from my voice and he smiles at me cheekily as we exit the car.

17

"I'll call you if I need you Gerry. Are you okay to be on standby tonight?"

"Sure am mate, on my lonesome tonight."

"Great, I'll let you know what's happening." He closes the door and gives the top of the car a slap.

As Gerry drives off, we walk towards the small shop front. It blends in with the other buildings and you would think it was a greasy spoon cafe. There is a queue outside, but Steven walks past them all and through the red door. We get some annoyed looks as we enter the building. The smell of garlic and herbs hits my nose and instantly makes my mouth water.

The interior of the restaurant is small and very cosy. There are six tables covered with white tablecloths and simple dark wood chairs. It is all very minimalistic but my God the food smells amazing.

As we stand in the doorway a young waitress comes over to us and hugs Steven. "Hi there honey, how are you?"

"Hi Rosa, I'm good. This is my girlfriend Gina." He introduces me and I immediately feel goose bumps form on my skin. His girlfriend. It sounds so nice coming out of his mouth.

Rosa holds out her hand. "Pleased to meet you Gina. Nice Italian name by the way."

"Nice to meet you too and I wish I could say it was Italian. It's actually short for Georgina. I think it's possibly Dutch."

"Well it's Italian tonight," she laughs and shakes my hand.

"Is he in tonight Rosa?" Steven asks.

"Yes, I'll go and tell him you're here. Take a seat."

We sit at the only empty table and Rosa disappears into the back.

"This place is nice, it's intimate isn't it," I say as I look around.

"Yes, it is. The food is amazing."

"I take it you come here a lot since the waitress knows you so well. Or do you own this place too?" I giggle but then I notice the smile on Steven's face.

"Oh, for goodness sake do you own the whole of Glasgow?"

He laughs. I shake my head and pour a glass of water from the jug on the table.

"Not the whole city but I do have my fingers in a lot of pies."

I almost choke on my drink.

"Oh, Gina get your mind out the gutter," he chastises me with a wicked grin on his face.

I'm still trying to deal with my flushed cheeks when a booming Italian voice with a hint of a Scottish accent comes from behind me. "Steven my boy. Looking good son."

Steven stands up and shakes the large hand of the

man standing beside our table. He looks like he could be in his late sixties.

"Ricco, looking good yourself."

"Ah you wee charmer. And who is this beautiful girl you've brought with you?"

"This is my girlfriend Gina."

"Ah…bellissima. Pleased to meet you Gina." He kisses the back of my hand. He is tall with silvery grey hair and I can tell he was a handsome man in his younger years.

"Pleased to meet you too Ricco. This is a cosy little place you have here."

"Thanks my dear but you can thank your good man here for the fact that it is still here at all. Right I'll get Rosa to get you drinks and a menu." He pats Steven on the back. "It's good to see you son."

"So, what happened with this place then?" I ask as we wait for Rosa to come back.

"I went to University with Ricco's grandson. Dario was one of my best friends at Uni. Rosa is Dario's wee sister. Ricco's daughter died when the children were very young. Her husband committed suicide and she eventually drank herself to death. Ricco and his wife basically brought the kids up."

"What happened to Dario?" I ask.

"When he was twenty-three, he was diagnosed with testicular cancer but by the time he had gone to see a doctor it was too late for them to help. His body was riddled with it. He passed away two years ago. Ricco went into a downward spiral and got into serious debt. The restaurant was going to be repossessed and I couldn't bear to see them suffer anymore. I offered to buy the place for them and sell it back when they were back on their feet."

"So, it's not actually yours then, you're only babysitting it."

"Well, no, it is mine. Ricco doesn't want to buy it back. He says the minute I offered to buy the place he felt ten years younger. I think he feels he's too old to handle the stress. We came to a compromise. I would buy it and be a silent owner and he would run the place without all the stress of being responsible for the bills."

"You're a good guy Steven you know that? So, what's the food like?" The smell of the cooking coming from the kitchen is making my stomach growl.

"Oh, the food is amazing. Ricco is a fantastic chef. He's from Sardinia originally and, like a lot of Italians, he was taught to cook by his family. The food is just so...." he pauses for a second and looks up slightly to his left as if he's trying to remember something.

I burst out laughing and hit such a fit of the giggles that I can't stop until the tears are streaming down my face.

Steven looks at me with amused bewilderment.

"Are you okay Gina? What's so funny?"

"Oh God Steven I am so sorry. You did Joey's 'Smell the Fart Acting'."

His puzzled expression stops my giggles dead.

"Please tell me you have watched Friends? Oh God I wish Charlie was here. We used to watch it constantly when we were at Uni. We'd do all-nighters and binge watch them. Aiden..." I stop talking. Even the mention of that bastard's name makes me want to throw up.

"Fuck it," I say under my breath.

"Friends was actually one of my favourites, but I only watched it because more often than not at least one of the girls had a good nipple shot. Jennifer Aniston was my favourite," he says with a huge smile. Expert of the U-turn.

I smile back. "Beast."

***

The food certainly outdid Steven's description. I now understand why this place is busy with a queue like an execution out the door. I sit back in my chair and place my hands on the table.

"Oh God Steven that was hands down the best Italian meal I have ever had, and I've been to Italy."

"I told you he was good didn't I?" He reaches across the table and takes both of my hands in his. "It's nice to see you smiling gorgeous." He runs his thumbs over my knuckles. "How do you fancy coming with me to find a Christmas tree for the house?"

"Really?"

"Yes really. I'm so sorry about earlier."

He gives me a little half smile.

"I'm going to make it up to you. We can get the tree tonight and we can go and get decorations for it tomorrow."

"Oh no we don't just decorate the tree. I'm going to make your house look like ten North Poles in one so when Santa visits, he'll think he's come home." I can't hide my excitement, I'm like a bloody child.

CHAPTER 3

"GINA HOW MUCH STUFF did you buy woman?"

I laugh to myself as I stand in the kitchen pouring us both a whisky cream liqueur. "Ehm, just enough."

I turn the bottle to read the label. It's not the run of the mill normal Bailey's Irish Cream. This one is from the Isle of Arran distillery. I've never tried a Scottish one before.

I put my phone into the dock in the kitchen and take the drinks back through to the living room where Steven is sitting in front of the empty tree completely surrounded by bags and boxes. I have to admit I did go a little over the top. Okay, I went massively out of control. I had to call Gerry three times yesterday when I was out shopping to come and pick up the bags for me because I couldn't carry them all at once. The tree we bought two days ago is huge so it will need lots of lights and tinsel and ornaments. I have a feeling that one and a half thousand lights may be a smidge too many though.

"Good God Gina we could power up the National Grid with these." He holds up the five boxes of lights and laughs.

"Ooh give me a minute. Don't move."

I say putting the filled glasses down on the table. I run upstairs and into the bedroom to grab my camera.

As I make my way back down to the living room, I hear the speakers come to life. Ah, Dean Martin, the epitome of cool. I stand at the living room door and watch as Steven fights with the hundreds of metres of tinsel.

Lifting the camera, I snap a picture of him. He looks up, a little startled, and a smile spreads across his face.

"What you doing missy?"

"I am documenting your best Christmas ever." I take another photo.

"Gina, do you know that you being here makes this my best Christmas ever? Come here." He pats the floor beside him. I go to him and sit down placing my camera on the floor in front of me. He kisses my shoulder then lifts his glass from the coffee table. The cold of the drink has caused condensation to form on the outside of the glasses. I lift mine and he raises his in a salute.

"To Gina, the saviour of my soul."

The ice cold, creamy whisky liqueur tastes like Christmas in a glass. I place it back on the table.

"Why do you say that Steven? That's what I should be saying to you. You know I wouldn't be here if it wasn't for you. I'd still be..."

And thanks to my darling daddy's words of advice to him my mouth is covered by Stevens as he kisses me and lowers me to the floor on top of all the tinsel planting little kisses between words on my lips; "You. Saved. Me." Lifting my camera Steven lies down beside me, smiles and says, "Christmas selfie."

We put our heads together and look at the camera as he clicks a photo and then three more.

I grab the camera and scroll through the photos. The first one has only Steven's torso and one of my boobs in it.

I show him it and he laughs. "I'll keep that one."

"Beast," I say without looking at him. I can feel him smiling. The second one at least has our faces in it, but I must have been in the process of blinking and I look drunk. The third one is really beautiful. We are both smiling and the tinsel behind us is a little out of focus, so it adds to the mood of the picture.

"This is good Steven, really good. If I am at all honest, I am a little jealous that you took it and not me."

"That's not all I'm good at gorgeous." Smiling at me, he turns and rises up over me, taking the camera from my hands and placing it on the coffee table. He runs his hand from my forehead, down the side of my face and on down to the hem of my t-shirt. Pulling it up over my head he proceeds to strip me naked. The feeling of the tinsel on my bare back and bum is a strange one. It is tickly on one hand but harsh on the other. He pulls a piece of tinsel from beside me and brings my arms up above my head. Oh my God he's tying my hands together with it. When he is done, he stands up and grabs the camera. Oh, shit no! I put my hands down and try to hide myself.

"Steven no please." I'm not up for being photographed naked. My body is far from photogenic.

"Why?"

"Oh, come on look at me."

He kneels down beside me and kisses my lips. "Gina you are the most beautiful woman I have ever been with do you know that? You have the body of a goddess. You are the picture of a perfect woman."

He pulls my hands down and puts them against his erection. "Do you think that happens for just anyone?"

I shake my head. Raising my hands above my head and stretching out my body. Steven smiles and starts snapping away

"For my eyes only babe," he says.

"Best."

Click.

"Christmas."

Click.

"Ever."

He puts the camera back on the table and pulls off his clothes in record time. Before I know it, he is down on the floor leaning over me. My hands are still tied with the tinsel and I keep them above my head as he takes one of my nipples in his mouth, sucking hard on it and nipping with his teeth every now and again. His cock is like hot steel against my leg. Having my hands tied is seriously arousing and, even though I know I could burst out of it at any time, not being able to move as freely as I would like intensifies everything. He leaves my nipple and trails little kisses down my body until his mouth reaches my very slick sex. He licks right up the slit and ever so slightly skims my clitoris. My body bucks under him.

"Mmm you taste so good Gina," he says his voice humming against me.

He licks again, this time a little harder, before he puts his tongue inside me. Oh God this is an amazing feeling. My hips rise of their own accord and he puts his hands on my thighs to hold me still. He licks again and then his tongue is replaced with two fingers. He moves them in and out and moves himself up so that he can kiss me. I can taste myself on his lips. It's so fucking hot and I am lost in our kiss, the sensation of his fingers arousing me, and I don't immediately notice he has put the tip of his penis inside me. I look at him with wide eyes. Is he really going to try this? Will it all fit?

"I'll take it slowly okay?" He has obviously gathered that I am little hesitant. "Relax, you'll like it."

I do as he says and relax the muscles I didn't realise I was clenching. As he slips in further, the feeling of stretching is sublime. He pushes right in and dips his head.

"Oh God Gina you have no idea what this feels like to me."

To me it feels like nothing I have ever experienced before. He removes his fingers and unties my hands. He takes one of my hands and eases my middle finger inside me. I can feel his cock. This is about as intimate as it gets and when he really starts to move, I am all but consumed. I can feel the orgasm build inside me and when I press my palm slightly over my clit I am done for. As I give in to my release, I feel Steven's body stiffen as he becomes thicker and hotter and eventually gives himself over and comes in heaving waves.

When we are both able to think again and I feel him

start to soften I try to remove my finger.

"No," he says. "Leave it there."

He removes himself and moves to the side of me. Placing his hand over mine he puts his finger back in. The feeling of his finger touching mine inside me is so hot and as he starts to move them together, I feel my body ready itself for another orgasm. My whole body is on fire and this time my climax is slower and more sensual than before. I'm wrecked. My limbs feel heavy.

"God Gina. You are fucking amazing." He kisses me so softly and I feel myself drift on the edge of sleep.

"Not so bad yourself," I say as I close my eyes and sleep consumes me.

***

What is that beeping noise? I open my eyes and notice the room is in semi darkness. Beep, beep, beeeeeeeeeeep.

"Fuck, Gina, what time is it." Steven jumps up off the floor.

We must have fallen asleep right here on the floor on top of the bloody tinsel of all things. He has a bit stuck to his bum cheeks. I can't help but laugh.

I grab my phone from the table and push the home button.

"Christ its quarter to four."

30

Beeeeeeeeeeeeeeeeeeeeeeeeeeeeeeeeeeeeeeep.

"That will be Charlie."

Tonight is the Winter Ball and Charlie and Mark are coming with us. We arranged for them to come over to get ready so that we could all leave together. As I get up off the floor my phone rings in my hand. Charlie's name appears on my screen.

"Hi honey." I answer.

"God almighty Gina will you open the damn door we are freezing our tits off out here."

"I'm sorry babe, I'm coming."

Steven lets out a little laugh beside me and I swat his arm.

"Come on up honey." I hang up and feel a little embarrassed.

"You might want to put on some clothes babe," Steven says, motioning to my completely naked body.

"You too, I love Charlie to bits, but I am not sharing that view with her."

He smiles and grabs his jeans from under the coffee table.

"Go and let them in, I really need to shower." I grab a throw from the couch, pull it round myself and make my way upstairs as Steven buzzes Charlie and Mark in.

I head in to the bathroom and start up the shower. Just as I am about to discard the throw the bedroom door flies open.

"Charlie you nearly gave me a heart attack there."

"Really? Feel my fucking hands." She comes over to me and puts both of her freezing cold hands on my upper arms. I let out a squeal.

"I am so sorry Charlie. We kind of fell asleep."

She looks at my messy hair and my flushed cheeks and laughs. "Yeah I can see that."

"Don't, I'm so embarrassed."

"Oh, don't be honey I'm only glad someone is getting some. So, was it good?"

"Oh, hell yes. Ever had sex on top of tinsel before?"

She slaps her hands over her ears and shouts, "Please don't say anymore and please, PLEASE do not put that tinsel on your goddamn tree."

"Sorry. Listen, I need to get showered. Your room is ready for you."

"Cheers honey. I'm going to go and get our bags from Gerry. I'll see you when you're done washing all the sex off you."

She turns and walks away muttering, "Lucky bitch," to herself.

CHAPTER 4

"WHAT DO YOU THINK babe?" Charlie asks twirling in front of me. The white maxi dress she has on is gathered under the ruched bust and flows over her bump. It has diamantes over the bust and on the straps. Her long blonde curls give her the look of Grecian goddess.

"Oh, Charlie you look beautiful."

"Not so bad yourself. Has Steven seen you in this dress yet?"

"No, I thought I'd surprise him. Can you help me with this necklace?"

"He's going to be a walking hard on when he sees you, it's stunning. Especially the fact that it barely covers your arse." She clips the necklace in place and smacks my behind.

"Right darling let's go and dazzle the men-folk."

As we make our way downstairs, we can hear Steven and Mark shouting. We exchange a puzzled look and when we reach the living room, we see the two of them standing in the lounge shouting at a rugby game on the T.V. Standing in the doorway we watch them for a few moments. They are both dressed in smart three-piece suits looking very handsome indeed.

"Are you kidding me? This game is shit. Do you think those girls will be ready yet?" Mark says to Steven.

"They're women. It's their prerogative to take their time," Steven replies.

Charlie clears her throat and their heads shoot round in tandem.

"Well that's a sight for sore eyes," says Steven as he walks towards me with purpose. He takes me in his arms and dips me back, kissing me as he does.

"Oh, get a fucking room you two," says Charlie with a look of mock disgust on her face.

As Steven lifts me up again, I see Mark walk towards Charlie. She holds up a hand.

"Do not even attempt it Mark. I'm so heavy you'll bloody drop me."

He doesn't stop. He walks right up to her, puts his hand behind her neck and leans in close. I hear him say, "You are a goddess you sexy mama."

Steven's phone pings. "Gerry is here. Are we ready

to go?"

"Sure are," Charlie says.

Sitting at the kerb is a limousine. I glance at Steven and he winks. "We will be arriving in style tonight."

Charlie looks about ready to pass out.

"You okay honey?" I ask.

"Never been in a limo before. Very excited babe."

Gerry gets out of the drivers' seat and comes around to open the doors.

"Evening folks." He is dressed in a chauffer's outfit with a hat and everything.

"Wow! Don't you look dapper Gerry," says Charlie.

He tips his hat. "Why thank you ma'am and, may I say you, look very beautiful tonight."

She giggles. "Oh, you old charmer you."

Steven and I sit on the back seat and Charlie and Mark sit along the side.

"Drink ladies?" Says Steven as the car pulls away. He produces a bottle of bubbly from the fridge.

"It's non-alcoholic," he says as he looks at Charlie who was, until a second ago, giving him the evil eye.

"Absolutely then."

***

The venue for the ball is a massive golf and spa resort outside Glasgow. As we pull up the sheer size and beauty of the place takes my breath away. There are twinkly lights on all the trees and the entrance archway. As we get out of the car, we are directed to the garden pavilion through a walkway flanked by little topiary trees with twinkling white lights. The place looks like a winter wonderland.

We walk through the doors and into a gaggle of people. There is a huge white balloon archway with a big banner above. It says Hopes and Dreams Winter Ball. The servers on either side offer us drinks. Steven and I take champagne and Charlie and Mark go for fresh orange. The place is buzzing and I wonder how I will ever find mum and dad. I needn't have worried about that though.

"Georgina, there you are darling."

Mum's voice sounds from behind me. I turn and give her a hug.

"Hi mum. You look fabulous. What happened to the dress we picked together? This isn't it."

She looks absolutely beautiful in her charcoal grey dress. It is a simple elegant dress with long sleeves and a plunging neckline, but it suits her figure beautifully. Her hair is pulled back in a messy bun and held in place by a little diamante clip. God she is still a stunning woman.

"Oh, don't even get me started on that. I had to send the bloody thing back, they sent me one two sizes too small. I nearly burst it trying it on. I'm fed up with Internet shopping you know they never get anything..." She doesn't get to finish as dad grabs her and kisses her. I look at Steven and we both laugh.

"God your mum and dad are hot stuff Gina," Charlie pipes up.

"For goodness sake Martin, not in front of your daughter," mum scolds him, dad laughs.

"Right you lot get to your seats, dinner will be served shortly. I've seen the menu and it looks amazing. There is also a surprise over at the big house later," she says.

"We will see you later for some dancing then," I say to her as we make our way to our table.

The theme of the evening is James Bond and the tables are all named after Bond films. It seems quite fitting since all the men resemble Bond in their suits.

"Which table are we at?" Asks Charlie.

"We are at The Spy Who Loved Me," says Steven, throwing me a little wink. I smile at him; the coincidence in the name is not lost on me.

"Ooh this is very exciting isn't it?" Charlie says, as she looks wide-eyed at all the bond themed decorations everywhere.

Our names are on black place cards with the little 007 logo on top. There is confetti scattered in the middle of the table, little guns and martini glasses, and the centrepiece on every table is a huge martini glass filled with fake ice and giant playing cards sticking out of the top.

There are four other women at our table. I don't know any of them, which is a blessing. Quite a lot of the people here are friends or acquaintances of my parents and I know at some point someone will ask awkward questions or give me a pitying look. The only other person who knows what that scumbag Aiden did, outside my friends and family, is Stan Mitchell, my solicitor. Everyone else will be shocked to see me with another man and I have a feeling some may be inwardly frowning upon our relationship. They would never say anything to my face. They are the sort of people to be all smiles and niceties, then as soon as you are out of earshot they are like those mean girls at high school.

Steven sits down beside me and immediately puts his hand on the bare skin of my back, just above where my dress sits. His hand is cool and it makes my skin tingle. I turn my face to him and can see in my peripheral vision two of the younger women talking to each other, unable to take their eyes off him. I smile a little wickedly and lean in to kiss him. I feel like a lioness marking my territory.

"Hmm. I don't care whose benefit that was for, it was nice," he whispers against my neck.

I hold my hand to my chest and try my best to look indignant. "I am sure I don't know what you mean."

He laughs and pours me a glass of water. "You're a naughty girl Gina."

CHAPTER 5

THE AFTER-DINNER ENTERTAINMENT in the grand ballroom of the estate house was fabulous. It had been converted into a casino and there were all sorts of games from Blackjack to Roulette tables and slot machines. Every single penny spent went straight to the charity because an anonymous business had paid for the venue and the Casino was donated free of charge by one of the big Casinos in Glasgow. We spent and lost a fortune too.

Afterwards, dancing commenced with gusto in the Garden Pavilion.

"I'm going to get a drink, do you want one?" I ask Steven.

"I'll have a whisky babe. I'm going to try and find your dad. I have something to run by him. I'll come and get you shortly." He leans in and plants a sweet soft kiss on my lips and I watch as he walks away a smile plastered all over my face.

When I am done ogling Steven's backside, I make my way to the bar. It is very busy and it takes a while for me to get noticed. The poor bartenders look absolutely shattered. I know the feeling. Charlie and I did a stint as bartenders when we were at Uni. It was great fun but incredibly hard work, especially when you had to deal with really drunk punters. As I place my drink order I hear my phone ping heralding the arrival of a text message. Pulling my phone out of my tiny excuse for a handbag I see Charlie's name on the screen.

Hey babe, where are you?

I tap out a reply.

At the bar.

She replies immediately.

Wait there I'm coming to you.

"Here you go darlin'. That'll be nine pound twenty-five."

Bloody hell that's expensive for two drinks. "They are really making good money here aren't they?" I say handing over a ten-pound note.

"You're not kidding," says the barman. "I normally work in the city centre and the prices there aren't as

41

high as this. I did hear that all the money made tonight on this bar is going to the charity because all the drinks were donated."

"That's a wonderful gesture. Keep the change then. Every penny helps. Thanks."

I lift the glasses and turn from the bar just in time to see Charlie appear behind me.

"Hey babe. Glad I found you, I swear I was about to kill someone in that toilet. I mean look at me." She gestures to her bump. "If a pregnant lady needs to pee, she needs to pee like NOW! Not when you are done chatting to your pal through the wall."

"I'm surprised you kept it together," I laugh at her.

"They eventually decided to take their little chat to the sink, right on time as well. I was about to go and use the men's. Poor Georgie was running out of room in here." She rubs her hands over her belly.

"Do you want a drink? I'm waiting on Steven coming back. He went to find my dad."

"I'll have a fresh orange honey. Steven and your dad are right over there." She gestures to the opposite end of the dance floor. "Mark is with them."

"God Gina my feet are killing me," Charlie sighs as we sit down with our drinks at an almost empty table. The only people sitting here are a rather amorous couple who seem totally oblivious to the fact that they are in a public place.

"You'll need to get Mark to give you a foot massage when we get back."

"Are you kidding? He's terrible at it. All he does is crush my foot bones. No, I just need to get out of these shoes. I really should have worn flats. I didn't want to look like a little fat munchkin, that's all."

"You're not fat and you're not a munchkin. You are carrying a little human inside you. That's a beautiful thing."

I almost choke on my drink at the expression on her face. "Oh, get me the sick bucket. Are you drunk?"

I am about to give her a sarcastic comeback when my gaze is drawn to where Steven, Mark and my dad are standing. They are not alone. There is a woman with them. She looks like she is possibly in her very early fifties. She is very glamorous and the way she holds herself oozes money. Her clothes and jewellery look extremely expensive. I watch them as they engage in their conversation and every time Steven says something, the woman laughs and touches his arm. I'm seething and I can't take my eyes off them.

"Gina are you okay?" Says Charlie.

"Yes." It's only when I answer her that I realise I have been clenching my teeth. I relax my jaw and look at her.

"What's up?"

"That," I say and motion towards the foursome.

Charlie watches for a moment then turns back to me.

"Gina, it looks like he knows her. I don't think you have anything to be worried about."

"I didn't worry about my goddamn husband and look what he did to me. Why is he letting her touch him like that? She's blatantly flirting with him. Can he not see that?" I pick up my gin and tonic and down what is left of it, then I drink Steven's whisky in one go. The burning in my throat brings tears to my eyes.

"Gina, he's not Aiden."

"How the hell do you know that Charlie? I don't know anything about him. I don't even know his damn date of birth or if he has a middle name or how many women he has been with before me." I know I am being irrational but it's true. I know next to nothing about this man. Our relationship has not been exactly straightforward so far and with everything that has gone on over the last few weeks we haven't had the time to really get to know each other.

"I'll tell you how I know that Gina shall I?" She says with a sly little smile on her face.

"Please enlighten me."

"Well his name is Steven. That's how I know he's not Aiden." She can't help herself and her smile gets wider. I shake my head and laugh as I close my eyes. This is why she is my best friend.

"Okay I give up," I say throwing my hands in the

44

air.

"Gina, I told you before, try it and see where it goes. I am telling you from an outsider's point of view, you two are great together. I've seen the way he looks at you when he doesn't think anyone else is looking. He adores you and I think it shows even more now that you have decided to actually start calling yourself his girlfriend. If you need to know stuff bloody well ask him. You've got a mouth. Now do you want to go and dance, I love this song."

I smile at her as the first few bars of 'I Will Survive' plays. "What about your feet?"

"I'm dancing in my bare feet. If I can't get my shoes back on, then Mark is simply going to have to carry me to the car. Now come on." She grabs my hand and we head to the dance floor.

We dance like teenagers, not giving a care as Gloria belts out her anthem. The words ring so true to me right now. Yes, I will survive, and it is thanks to the people I now hold so dear to me. It's great to be carefree for a little while and as the song finishes, I grab Charlie and hug her tight.

"I love you my darling Charlie, you keep me sane."

"I love you too babe, but I think someone wants to cut in."

I let her go as Steven catches me around the waist. "Hey gorgeous," he says as he spins me round and kisses me.

"Come and dance with me."

I look at Charlie who winks at me and smiles. Steven pulls me to him as the slow and sultry voice of Norah Jones sweeps us away. He holds my right hand over his heart and I put my left on his shoulder. His moves are so fluid and I am quickly lost in the rhythm of us. I can feel his heart beat through his clothes and I lay my head against his shoulder. We are so close to each other I can feel his body heat right through my dress and I can't think of anywhere I would rather be than in his arms.

As the song comes to an end, I look up at him and into his beautiful blue eyes.

"Thank you gorgeous," he says and leans down to kiss me.

We stay like that for ages even as the next song starts, even though the music is a fast and pumping dance beat. He smiles against my lips as we are told to 'get a room' by some very drunk party people.

"Come on let's find Charlie and Mark before we get arrested."

"And why would we get arrested may I ask?"

He leans down and whispers in my ear. "You're not generally allowed to fuck in public."

He takes my hand and leads me off the dance floor as if he hasn't just set my knickers on fire.

CHAPTER 6

SUNDAY MORNINGS WERE ALWAYS a favourite of mine when I was at University. It was either the day after a big piss up or just a lazy day. I want this particular Sunday to be a bit of both. The Winter Ball went fantastically last night. Between the casino, the bar, donations and the late-night auction the charity was able to raise just over half a million pounds. We didn't stay for the auction, but mum told me there were some amazing things up for grabs; holidays, cars and the like. She said this was the first year they have had an auction and it was such a success they were going to try it for all of the events through the year.

It is still dark outside and my phone says it is only five thirty in the morning. As usual I am in bed alone. Steven came to bed with me last night and there was a half-hearted attempt at something sexy, but we decided against it when I fell out the bed and Steven tripped over the duvet trying to help me up. We lay in bed giggling until I fell asleep. I don't know how long he stayed with me. What I do know right now is that I really need to pee, and my mouth is dry and stinky. I make my way to the bathroom and grab Stevens robe from the back of the door.

When I have tended to my full bladder and yucky mouth, I make my way quietly downstairs. The blue glow of the TV lights up the closed glass panel doors of the TV room. Steven must be in there, but I don't want to disturb him. I tiptoe towards the door and hear a muted one-sided conversation. He is on the phone. I know I shouldn't, but I stop and listen.

"Are you kidding me? God that fucking deceitful bitch. Have the police been to see her?"

There is a pause as the person on the other end talks.

"And they are positive she wrote it? I take it they did handwriting analysis."

Another pause.

"So when will he be released then?

Pause.

"Fuck so soon. I really didn't want to have to deal with this again. We need to keep tabs on him Nick."

Nick. I remember him talking to a Nick the night I went home and my bedroom had been trashed by

Abby.

"Will he have different licence conditions this time? I really don't want him anywhere near Glasgow. Especially not now."

Oh God, his bloody dad is being released from prison!

"Okay Nick I'll call you later on, just see what you can find out before then."

Pause.

"Great thanks." I hear him sigh loudly. "Fucker," he says softly.

I scurry away from the door and onto the second step pretending I'm just coming downstairs as he opens the door. He is only wearing a pair of grey pyjama trousers.

"Hey babe, what you doing up so early?"

"I really needed to pee." I smile at him trying my best to make my face remain impassive. I really hope he talks to me about it and doesn't try to deal with this by himself.

"Are you naked under that robe Gina?" His voice is low and his breathing shallow.

"Why don't you find out?"

He scoops me up and carries me into the kitchen where he deposits me on the kitchen table.

Pulling the belt loose he opens the front of the robe, sucking in a breath as he sees my nakedness beneath it.

49

Without speaking he sits in the chair in front of me, grabs my robe and slowly slides me off the table until I'm standing in front of him. As he frees himself from his trousers, I notice that that is *all* he is actually wearing. He is getting me so turned on that I can barely wait. I move myself so that I'm standing right over him, my legs on either side of his. He swipes a finger right up my sex and skims my clit. The heated sensation travels through my nervous system and I feel goose bumps form all over my body. Grabbing my hips, he guides me down onto him. I sit still for a moment and he flexes his cock inside me hitting that sweet spot that sends shivers right through me. I move up and down on him and he takes my hands linking our fingers. I get into a rhythm and very quickly feel my muscles ready themselves for an orgasm. As it washes over me, I keep my gaze locked with Steven's. I'm utterly mesmerised by him and that makes it all the more intense. His blue eyes are stunning and I feel them bore into my soul. As I come down from my high, I start to move again to get him there and as I feel him thicken and his body stiffen, I give a little squeeze as I pull up and push down on him. His fingers grip mine tighter, but he never takes his gaze from mine. His own orgasm takes him and his hips jerk against mine and still we stare at each other, each of us slightly in awe.

When we are both spent, he pulls my head down

and kisses me with a sense of urgency, as if he is trying to expel something from within his soul. When he lets my lips go, he holds his face close to me, our noses touching.

"Special girl," he whispers against my lips. We stay like that for a long time until he starts to go limp and we become rather slippery.

"Come with me." He leads me to the downstairs bathroom and closes the door. He opens the little cupboard under the sink and takes out a washcloth. Running the hot water, he soaks it and wrings it out and I watch as he ever so gently cleans me up. He cleans himself and when he is done, he wraps the robe round me and ties the belt in front. He cups the side of my face and runs his thumb over my lips.

"Are you okay?" He asks softly.

I nod. "Yes, very."

"Me too," he says as he places a soft kiss on my lips. "Want some coffee?"

"Yes please."

We head to the kitchen and I sit down at the table pulling my legs up and resting my feet on the chair, my arms wrapped around my shins.

"So last night was fun huh? I went to last year's Winter Ball but this one was much better and they raised a lot more money this time."

He is talking with his back to me as he busies

himself making coffee.

"It was fun yes."

He turns and frowns at my dead tone. "What's wrong?"

"Well...." My words are stuck in my throat.

Steven pours the coffees and comes to sit opposite me at the table. "Tell me, what's wrong Gina? Please. If I've done something to upset you, I need to know."

"No, you haven't done anything wrong Steven. It's just... last night gave me a wakeup call."

"About what? Us?" His concerned expression makes me feel bad and I reach over and hold his hand. It's warm.

"Yes, but not in the way you're thinking. I was sitting with Charlie while you were talking with my dad and I was watching you. I saw that woman who was there with you and how she was desperately flirting with you."

Steven cocks his head to the side with a bemused look on his face. "I'm sorry Gina I didn't even notice." His expression grows softer.

"Do you know her well? She looked like she knew you." I can't hide the jealousy in my voice and I hate it

"Her name is Estelle Montague. She owns casinos and nightclubs in quite a few cities in the UK. She's a serious money-maker. But she never moved away from her roots in Glasgow. I admire that."

I get that he admires that. From the little I actually do know about him it seems as though he always tried to return to his roots since he ended up back in the Scottish care system after being taken into care in London.

"She set up the casino at the venue last night. She does a lot of fundraising for various charities and her casinos are always a big hit. I've been to a few functions where she has set them up." He takes a drink of his coffee and I do the same. "What did you see?"

"She was laughing at everything you said and every time she laughed, she touched you."

"Were you jealous Gina?" He has a slight smirk on his face and it is starting to piss me off.

"Get that fucking smile off your face Steven. God." I have raised my voice a little and I can't look at him. I lower my gaze and shake my head.

"Hey come on, I'm sorry." He shifts his chair closer to me and takes my hands in his.

"Look at me Gina," he says as he puts a finger under my chin so that I'm looking at him. "You have to tell me what's going on."

"Okay," I say and take a deep steadying breath. "I did get a little jealous but more than that I got worried. No."

I hold up a finger when I see him about to speak.

"You have to let me finish okay."

He nods and I continue.

"I got worried because my head is messed up Steven. I hear you when you say you would never do what that bastard did, but there is always something there in the back of my mind. You know I had a hard time even convincing myself that you would want to be with me in the first place. Finding out what he did set me back a million times further."

I take a gulp of coffee and release my other hand from Steven's. I hold the mug close to me, trying to pry some comfort out of its heat. He sits back in his chair and mimics me.

"I came to the realisation last night that I don't really know you that well at all. I mean I know about the most traumatic time of your life before I even know your damn date of birth. That's a pretty backwards way of having a relationship don't you think?"

He nods but stays quiet allowing me to go on.

"What I am trying to say here is that I don't know if you are capable of hurting me or not and it scares me. I can't go through that again Steven, I just can't. You can sit here and tell me you won't do that till the cows come home and I know somewhere in my heart that I believe you, but it doesn't stop me from worrying constantly."

I close my eyes and the tears I didn't know were

forming fall from my lids. As I open them again, I see Steven put his mug down on the table. He pulls me off the chair and into his lap, his strong arms wrapping around me.

"Gina I am in this for real, okay? I understand why you would think that, you'd have to be a robot not to be affected by what happened to you. Please believe me when I say I would never hurt you like that. I would never hurt anyone like that."

I lay my head in the crook of his neck. "I believe you," I whisper.

"Let's go somewhere more comfortable." When we are in the hallway, I think we are heading for the TV room but instead he leads me upstairs.

When we reach the bedroom, he kicks the door closed and takes the robe off me. "Get back in bed."

I do as I'm told and watch as he strips out of his trousers and gets in beside me. We lie down facing each other but not touching.

"Right gorgeous fire away. What do you want to know? This works both ways by the way. I need to know the same things about you."

I'm fine with that, I have nothing to hide. Well maybe my age but he already knows that.

"Okay let's start with your date of birth," I say with a smile.

"Second of August eighty nine. What's yours?"

"The twentieth of March eighty-six. Do you have a middle name?"

"No. Do you?"

"Yes, Isabelle. After my gran. What's your favourite animal?"

"A lion. What's yours?"

I laugh. "That makes sense. Mine is an owl. What's your favourite film?"

"The Great Escape. What's yours?"

"A Streetcar Named Desire." I give a shy little smile and avert my eyes for a second. When I look at him again, he is smiling. He caught that look.

"Why did you look away from me Gina?"

"No reason. So how..."

"No, you don't Gina, you're blushing. Tell me why," he butts in. There's no getting away from this. Damn my tell-tale face.

"Okay. The first time I saw you, you know when I knocked you down the stairs, I thought you had a kind of young Marlon Brando bad boy look about you. He was damn hot when he was younger."

"Oh right, yes I suppose he was. Do you think I'm hot Gina?" He laughs as he asks me that.

I pick up one of the small cushions off the bed and whack him with it. "You know fine well you are a hottie, stop trying to embarrass me by making me say it."

"Okay, okay sorry where were we."

"Thank you. I was about to ask how many women you have been with?"

He sucks in a breath through his teeth. "That's a big question Gina are you sure you want to ask that?"

"Yes." I'm not really but I need to get to know him better if I want to be able to trust him.

"Okay seventeen."

That's more than I had imagined it would be. "Were they serious?"

He shakes his head. "I'm not answering that until you tell me how many men you've been with. That was the rule remember."

"Okay, including you, five."

I see his jaw tick ever so slightly. It makes me smile. This has annoyed him slightly but he's trying not to show it. Strangely, I like that he might be a little jealous.

"So, were any of those women serious?"

"Only two. The first one was when I had just started Uni. We were stupid kids just out of high school. Her name was Leah. She proposed to me and I said yes just because I didn't want to hurt her feelings."

Oh my God he was engaged. I just figured he had flitted from woman to woman like a Casanova. "Did you love her?"

"I don't think so. I think I wanted to, but she was a

bit of a bitch actually. She loved herself way too much and always got annoyed if she wasn't the centre of attention. We lived in the same student house in the city centre along with four other people. Anyway, it only lasted about four months. She quit Uni before the first year was over to work as an au pair in New York. She dumped me by email the day she left. I can't say I was saddened. Actually, I think I was relieved."

"God that's cold. She does sound like she was a bitch. Lucky escape there then eh? So, who was the other serious one?"

He smiles at me. "She *is* you Gina."

My breath catches in my throat and I actually think my heart stops. "W-what?"

Steven puts his hand to my face. "She is you Gina," he says again. You are as serious as I have ever let myself get. You are the only woman I have been with that I've ever trusted to tell what happened when I was a boy. You don't know everything, but you will. I'm not ready to tell you the rest yet. I want to enjoy us for a while first. Is that okay?"

"Of course it is. Steven I really don't know what to say. I think this is something very special too, but I had no idea you felt that way about me."

"I'm in love with you Gina. You astound me. You make me want to be a better person. You make me want to go to the ends of the earth to protect you." He puts his hand in my hair and pulls my mouth to his, his kiss is so soft and tender and I'm totally lost in this beautiful moment. We make sweet slow love to each other until sleep consumes us both and the world floats away for a few hours.

CHAPTER 7

THE SUNLIGHT PEEKING ROUND the blinds is bright and I wonder to myself what time it is. I am lying on my side and Steven is tucked in so close behind me that it feels as though we are fused together. He has his hands over both of my breasts and every so often he gives a little squeeze. I think he must be asleep because his breathing is even and rhythmic. It feels like this is where I should be, where I should always have been. He flexes his hands again but this time he pushes his hips into me and I feel that he has a little touch of morning glory.

"Morning gorgeous," he says as he nuzzles into my neck.

"Morning yourself." I turn so that I am facing him. "Do you think we should get up? What time is it?"

Steven reaches over to the bedside table and grabs

my phone. "Wow! It's ten forty. We must have slept for hours." He hands the phone to me. "Here, you have a text from your mum. I'm going for a shower."

He leans over and kisses my forehead as he gets out of bed and heads for the bathroom giving me a glorious view of his magnificent arse. I open the text message.

Hi darling. Thanks for coming last night it was so nice to see you having fun. Check out the pictures. Call me when you are able. Xx

I smile at the screen. I'm glad we went last night too. It really was a brilliant night. I flick open the Facebook app on my phone and go to the Hopes and Dreams charity page. The whole thing is awash with pictures and comments from last night. I tap on the pictures and start looking through them. There are hundreds and a lot of the people I don't even know.

I come across some photos that were taken in the Casino and find one in particular of the four of us at the roulette table with Charlie throwing her hands in the air. She did win on that once. Then she bet the lot and lost it on the next go. The next picture shows her with her head in her hands and the rest of us consoling her but laughing at the same time. It is such a candid set of photos and we all look so young and carefree. We really did scrub up well.

I flick through a load more and find one of Steven,

my dad and Mark, obviously taken when they were chatting. This one is posed and they all look very handsome in their suits. The next one has them standing talking and that woman is there, Estelle that was her name. She is laughing a little too enthusiastically for my liking. I knew she was beautiful from a distance but up close you really can see she is a stunning woman. What I do notice, and it calms me slightly, is a diamond ring on her finger. God, it is huge. Maybe she was only being friendly with Steven last night. Damn, I really wish I could get a grip and get over this. Jealousy does not sit well with me.

I hear the shower go quiet and a moment later Steven emerges from the bathroom with a towel around his waist, his upper body glistening with little beads of water. Oh yummy.

"Oi get your tongue back in your mouth," he says with a wicked little smile as he struts around the room. I get up from the bed and pick up a pillow launch it at his back and run giggling into the bathroom, locking the door behind me.

"Keep laughing babe, naughty girls get punished."

Oh dear God the way he says that makes me clench my thighs tightly together. "Stop that I'm going to need a cold shower at this rate."

"I'm making coffee so don't be in there long," he

says, and I hear the bedroom door open and close as he leaves me a quivering mess.

***

"Morning sleepy head number two," says Charlie as I walk in to the kitchen. She is sitting at the table with her bare feet in Mark's lap. "Well we were actually up at the back of five this morning, but we decided to go back to bed."

"Need to know basis Gina, need to know and I don't need to know," she laughs holding up her hand.

"Coffee gorgeous?" Steven asks and I look over to where he is standing. He is dressed in perfectly fitting jeans and a tight white t-shirt. He turns and smiles at me. Oh, he knows exactly what he is doing. He obviously remembered my favourite film comment. He certainly has that bad boy look of Stanley Kowalski going on this morning. And I like it. A lot.

"Yes please. So guys what's the plan for today?" I ask Charlie and Mark as I sit at the table with them.

"We are off to see Mark's parents today."

Says Charlie. Mark smiles.

"Yeah, we are going to drop off their Christmas pressies because they are deserting us on Tuesday. Pair of lucky gits are going on a Caribbean cruise for three weeks over Christmas and New Year."

Charlie leans over and pats Mark's leg. "Don't

worry babe we've got each other."

"Aww…get a room you two," I laugh at her.

"Well I have decided that we need to finish the Christmas decorations today."

Charlie snorts and I flash her a 'don't say a word' look. She smiles and shakes her head. I'm sure the tinsel will be fine. The living room is still strewn with decorations and the tree is still bare. It will give us something fun to do and will hopefully take Steven's mind off that phone call he had this morning. I hope he tells me about it. I know he thinks he needs to handle everything on his own because that's what he has always done but maybe I can make him realise he's not alone anymore, that he can lean on me if he needs to.

"Are you going as mad as your mother with the decorations?" Charlie asks.

"I have bought rather a lot, but I don't think I could beat mum. She could probably get into the Guinness Book of Records with hers."

"Carla is Christmas daft," Charlie says to Mark. "I remember thinking of National Lampoons Christmas Vacation the first Christmas I spent at Gina's house. I swear you can see the house from the train station."

"Yeah, dad has basically just given up even asking what she has bought next. She would keep the stuff up all year if she could get away with it."

"My mum and dad put up a tree and a wreath on the door and that is it. My brother and I used to love going to our grandparents house because it always looked so much more Christmassy," says Mark.

Steven comes to the table and puts a mug of coffee down in front of me and takes the seat beside me. When Charlie starts talking about her Christmas experiences and how it was summer in South Africa at Christmas for her, I glance at Steven and notice that he is staring into space. A little muscle ticks in his jaw but he stays perfectly still. It is getting uncomfortable to see him like this. While we all talk about our wonderful family Christmas experiences he is sitting there listening and remembering he had none of that.

I change the conversation as best I can so that it doesn't look too obvious. "So, Valentine's day will be coming up soon guys. What are you two going to be doing?"

Charlie gives me a little smile before she answers. She understands the situation. "Well I'm due this little one on the twenty first of February so I'm probably going to be sitting on the couch like a beached whale. There isn't going to be any sexy time for us on Valentine's."

"Aww don't worry there's always after." I smile at her.

"Yeah when we have not slept for forty-eight hours

and an orgasm is the only way to get to sleep," she laughs. "We better get ready to go sweetness. We said we would be over at your parent's house for three," she says to Mark as she puts her feet on the floor. Steven laughs.

"Well folks, Gerry is going to be here in about half an hour to take you wherever you need to go and I'm taking my woman out for lunch." Good it worked. He is smiling again.

CHAPTER 8

THE SOFT STRAINS OF the piano play through the speakers in Steven's office. This music, that I now know to be *'Nuvole Bianchi'* by Ludivico Einaudi, reminds me of when we first met. He played it in his car and I loved it so much that any time I hear it now I think of Steven and it makes me smile. I have been doing a lot more of that over the last day or two. As much as he doesn't think it, he really does make me happy.

Right now, Steven is working at his desk and I am sitting on his sofa looking through a load of pictures I took at the park yesterday. The weather was lovely, all crisply frosty and sunny. I got some great shots and it was so good to get out and use my new camera. It is, without doubt, the best purchase I have made in a long time. My new apartment will be my next. I will be completing on that as soon as possible after New Year. I finally decided on the one in the Italian Centre in the Merchant City area of Glasgow. It's part of getting my life back. What better way to spend the life insurance of a cheating bastard husband than to buy myself a new house? Steven has said I can stay with him until it's ready. I love being with him. It is nice to know I am not on my own anymore.

As I sort through the photos I start playing with little strands of my hair. Pulling my elastic out of it I give my scalp a rub, closing my eyes to savour the sensation. When I open them, I am met with the beautiful blue gaze of Steven looking at me over the top of his laptop with a smile on his face.

I frown at him and cock my head to the side. "What?" I ask.

"Are you kidding me? That was quite a little show there Gina. Got me all hot and bothered."

"Oh shut up I was only rubbing my head for God sake. You're such a sex pest," I laugh, tying my hair back up.

"Oh…I'm a sexy pest, thanks for that little term of endearment darling."

"No not sexy pest, sex pest. Well you are sexy but that's not what I mean, oh just shut up," I say and go back to my screen, my cheeks a little redder than before.

When I look back up at him, he is staring at his screen with a cute smile on his face and he's obviously trying to stave off some giggles at my expense. I smile at him then go back to what I was doing and I catch him in my peripheral vision looking at me. When I see him look away, I look back up at him. We do this for the next few minutes and each time the smiles on our faces get wider until we are both in hysterics.

When we have calmed down enough to speak, I ask him what he is working on.

"A project for a Japanese client. They are building new premises in Seattle. I'm actually submitting some plans to them today and then I will wait to hear whether they want me to tender to be the architect on the project."

"Were those the people you were meeting with last week?"

He nods.

"What a wonderful job you have. That sounds so exciting," I say a little in awe of him.

"Yeah, it was for a while but as soon as I got into property developing as opposed to designing, I knew that was more what I wanted to do. I own a lot of commercial properties in the city. Some of them I run myself and others I rent to other businesses. If this job with the Japanese firm falls through it wouldn't be too big a deal to me. I have a few other projects I'm working on right now."

"You're very flippant about the architecture side of your work. Why didn't you say no to this company if you don't really want to do it?"

"Oh, don't get me wrong, I do want the job but if I land it it'll mean I have to be away for a few weeks at a time."

"You mean in Seattle?" I get a little pang in my chest.

"Yes. I don't know how long exactly but it would probably have to be two or three weeks at a time over the course of the project. Right now, if I get shortlisted, I will have to go and assess the site to ensure it's viable to build on."

This is such a bad thing to think, but right now I'm hoping he doesn't get it. I don't want him to be away from me for too long. Ugh I'm so selfish.

"When will you know?"

"It won't be until the start of January, but as soon as I get the call I will have to go. The first visit will only be for a few days and even then, I'm not guaranteed to get the contract."

"Okay." I jump a little when my phone pings next to me. It's my appointment reminder for my therapy session. Saved by the bell.

"Is that your appointment with Nate?"

"Yes, it's in half an hour but since it is going to take

me literally less than two minutes to get there I don't need to leave right now."

"I'll walk down with you. I have to go in to the office to send off these plans. I need to speak to Nate anyway," he says as he closes his laptop.

"Right, I'm going to get changed. I'll get you downstairs in five okay?" I close my laptop, pack it away and head towards the door. Steven does the same and as I walk out the door, he slaps me right on my bum cheek. When I turn around in shock, he winks at me. I can't do anything else but laugh.

"Sex pest," I shout and run to the bedroom.

***

We leave Steven's building and head towards Royal Terrace. There is a companionable silence between us as we walk side by side. Every few steps Steven's hand brushes mine and each time it gets more pronounced. After about four or five little touches he grabs my hand and links our fingers together. The suddenness of it shocks me a little but also makes me smile. Pulling our hands upwards he kisses my knuckles. He swings our hands between us as we walk, and I turn my head and look at him. He doesn't look back at me, but he has a huge smile on his face. If this moment could be frozen in time, I would have to say it would rank up there with the few simply perfect moments I have had in my life.

A lot of the perfect moments I thought I had experienced while I was married are slowly falling away. It is a whole decade of my life that I would now rather forget. Today is going to be the start. My counselling sessions with Nate are about to change. I had been seeing him for grief counselling but that changed when I found out what Aiden had done. My session last week was mostly made up of me telling Nate everything that had gone on since I had last seen him. He told me he was going to work out a plan for me and that the next session would be the start of something very different.

As we reach the front of Steven's office building, I expect him to let go of my hand, but he doesn't. He keeps his fingers linked through mine and we make our way inside. We head upstairs and when we reach his floor, I try to remove my hand, but he doesn't let go.

"I'm coming up with you," he says.

"Why?" I say my tone a little too inquisitive.

"Because I need to speak to Nate, I told you that. Don't worry I'm not going to gate-crash your session if that's what you are worried about."

"No, I didn't think that at all. It's just..."

I can't seem to get out what I'm trying to say. He stops us halfway up the last flight of stairs.

"Gina, I don't care if people see us together. I want everyone to know you are my girl. Do you think people will think less of you because you are moving on with your life?"

"This is not going to be an easy process for me Steven. You have to believe me when I say I am happy we are together, but this is a big thing for me. I know Nate will help me and this time I will let him. I want this to work."

I can feel tears threatening my eyes and it is taking a lot of willpower to stop them.

"Let's go," I say and pull his hand as I head up the stairs.

We walk in to the reception area of Nate's office and Fiona looks up, her ever-present smile widening when she sees me.

"Oh, hi Gina you're early," she says and puts her head back down only to lift it again as she double takes my hand in Steven's.

"Oh h-hi Steven." She looks at us quizzically for a few seconds then she gives me a nod and a wink. What a great, professional doctor Nate is. Fiona obviously knows nothing about us. It must be hard for him not to discuss certain things with his wife.

"Nate won't be long Steven, he said you were coming in to see him today."

"Yes, I have something to run by him."

"Oh, I don't want to know. Knowing you two it will be rugby or car related. That's where my brain switches off. Take a seat. Do either of you want a coffee?"

We both decline and her phone rings so we take a seat and wait.

Nate's door opens and a young girl walks out. She must be in her mid-teens and her eyes are red rimmed. I feel for Nate. He spends the whole day with crying people. It's so nice to know that Fiona has such a sunny outlook on life; she probably keeps him sane. He gives us a one-finger gesture to let us know he won't be long and walks over to Fiona with the girl. They talk for a moment and then he comes to us.

"Well isn't this a nice sight. How are you mate?" He says to Steven as they both shake hands.

"Yeah good, do you have a couple of minutes?"

"Absolutely. Gina grab a cuppa, I'll be with you shortly okay." I nod to him as Steven stands up and follows him in to his room.

I wonder for a moment what he has to talk to Nate about and then I remember the phone call he was having when I got up on Sunday morning. That is probably what it is about. He has still not told me anything and it is a little frustrating. I think he has probably spent so long not having anyone to tell things to that he finds it hard to share information with me, even when it could affect my safety. God we really do have a lot of work to do to make our relationship work.

I am a little lost in my thoughts that I don't immediately notice them coming out of the office.

I get a little fright when Nate says, "Right Gina your turn."

Steven leans in to me and gives me a chaste kiss on the lips. "Come down to my office and get me when you are done here okay?"

"Okay," I say as he walks out the door saying a goodbye to Fiona as he goes. I follow Nate in to his office with a mixed sense of purpose and trepidation.

CHAPTER 9

AS I SIT ON the sofa opposite Nate, the silence engulfs me. He is sitting smiling at me and I look at him confused.

"What?" I say.

"I'm very proud of you Gina."

"Ehm, thanks. But why?"

"You've done a complete turnaround with your life. You didn't let all the things that happened affect you negatively. I was worried that after everything you found out you would go back into yourself again and not see the good that could come from such a personal tragedy. So yes, I am proud of you and as I said before Steven is a good guy."

"Well thanks." I don't know what else to say.

"So, let's get on with this then. I'm going to give you a rundown of what is going to be discussed at the next set of sessions and we will start properly next time. This is going to give you the chance to give your input about what you would like to go over as well as what I think we need to work on. Okay?"

"Yes that's fine." I can already tell this is going to help me get over everything and finally lay a lot of ghosts to rest.

***

The door to Steven's office is closed and when I try the handle it is locked. That's strange. I've only been up there for an hour and he told me to come back down and get him when I was done. I pull my phone from my bag to call him and see a text. When I open the message and read the words I gasp.

Go straight back to the house after your appointment. Lock the door and don't answer it to anyone xx

Oh my God. I read it over and over again, trying my best to process what I'm seeing. I'm scared. What the hell has happened and where is he? I tap out a reply.

I'm worried Steven will you please call me. I'm on my way home now.

I hit send and put my phone back in my bag. I make my way back to the house double quick.

As soon as I'm through the door, I lock it and head

straight for the kitchen. I pull a bottle of whisky from the cupboard with shaking hands and grab a glass. I am shaking so much that the glass clinks as I try to set it down on the worktop. I fill the glass with at least three measures and knock the whole lot back in one go. The burning of the alcohol makes my eyes water. I open my bag and check my phone. Nothing.

The house is eerily quiet right now. I know in my heart this has something to do with that phone call he took about his dad. I mean I didn't get the start or the other end of the conversation, but it doesn't take a genius to figure out what is going on here. I'm a little angry at him for not telling me about it. I get that he feels this is something he needs to deal with on his own. He has had to do that all his damn life. I have to make him see that I'm here for him, that he is not alone anymore. I write another text to him and send it off.

I'm home and the door is locked. Will you please let me know you are ok? I'm scared.

I grab the bottle of whisky and head upstairs to shower.

***

The mattress dips beside me and my eyes shoot open. Steven is sitting in front of me and I look at him through screwed up eyelids. He looks dreadful.

"Oh my God Steven where have you been? What is

going on?" My voice is hoarse, still laden with sleep, and it takes a moment for my eyes to adjust in the bright light of the bedside lamp. He has a cut on his cheek and a bruise forming round it. I gasp in shock.

"Steven what happened to you? God."

I reach up to touch him and he flinches back.

"I'll explain, I need to get showered first."

He lifts the bottle of whisky from the bedside table and drinks a huge swig from it.

Steven puts his hand out and touches my face. "Sweet girl," he whispers.

He gets up off the bed and heads for the shower taking the whisky with him. He takes another large drink from the bottle and kicks the door shut behind him.

I hear the water pattern change and I know he is now under the spray. I feel the sudden urge to go to him. There is something really sad about a person who thinks he doesn't need anyone's help, but I know different. Everybody needs someone in some way. I open the bathroom door and strip off my clothes. As I open the shower door Steven turns and stares at me with wide eyes but doesn't stop me. I step in and barely have time to close the door before I'm caught in his hold. His lips crash onto mine as the hot water pours over our heads. He is holding me so tight it is as though he thinks I might float away if he doesn't tether me to him. The kiss is hard and bruising. He bites my bottom lip so hard I swear I can taste blood, but I don't care, he needs this. Something bad has happened; I know it. His body is so tense and wound like a coiled spring and I know he needs a release from it.

Steven bows his head and rests his forehead against mine. He doesn't speak and his eyes stay closed. I reach my hand up and caress his face where he is hurt. He flinches slightly but doesn't pull away from me. He lifts me up and pushes my back against the cool wall. Before I can even think he is inside me. He moves fast. A little too fast. His movements are hitting me so deep and in any normal situation I would revel in it but not this time. This time it is just for him. I know even when he comes, he won't enjoy it. He is trying to expel something and I am merely a vessel for that in this moment.

As he finds his release, he almost screams my name followed by a loud "fuck!" He keeps me pinned against the shower wall for a few moments, all the while his body wracks in huge heaves as he tries to regain some composure. As he slowly lets me down, he puts his head next to mine and whispers.

"Sorry."

"Don't apologise please Steven. I want you to promise me you will tell me everything when we get out of here okay?"

He nods. I grab the shower gel from the shelf. Running my soapy hands over his perfectly sculpted torso I feel his muscles begin to give a little. He stands still and lets me wash him.

I dry myself off, pull my hair up in a towel and get dressed in a t-shirt and leggings. Steven wraps a towel around his waist and sits down on the bed with his head in his hands.

"Tell me what happened Steven, please?"

He shakes his head. "I don't even know where to start Gina. I don't even really know what is going on myself to be honest."

"Steven, I heard you on the phone on Sunday morning. I gathered enough from what I heard to know he is back in the picture."

He turns his head and looks at me. I see relief in those beautiful troubled eyes. "Why didn't you tell me you had heard it?"

"I was trying to give you the opportunity to tell me yourself Steven. You have to get used to the fact that I'm here. We are in an actual relationship. That means sharing things with each other. It doesn't matter how trivial we think it might be, we have got to communicate with each other."

I put my hand on his and give a little squeeze. "Tell me what the phone call was about."

He clears his throat and takes a deep breath. "Okay.

I didn't go to sleep after the ball. I stayed with you until you fell asleep and then I went back downstairs. I had a wee chat with Charlie actually. She was still up but Mark was in bed. He was wasted. She is very funny your friend. She said she was considering raiding your bag so she could steal two tampons to stick up his nose because he was snoring."

I laugh and shake my head. "Yes, that's Charlie, she says it like it is."

"So, after she eventually went to bed, I took my iPad into the TV room to deal with some emails. That's when I found a message from Nick."

"Sorry to interrupt but who is this Nick? I heard you say his name on the phone at my house as well."

"He's a good friend who runs a private security company. They deal with all sorts of security from personal data security to hiring out personal bodyguards and door staff. He has been doing security work for me for the last two and a half years and was the one who first alerted me to the release of my father."

He says the word father through gritted teeth and clenches his fists. I rub his knuckles and try my best to reassure him.

"I've since found out that the reason he was released at all was because he had been given a term of imprisonment. When he was first sentenced his imprisonment was a life sentence. There was no tariff on the sentence like there is with life terms now. You know how you hear on the news, 'life in prison with a minimum of so many years'."

I nod and allow him to carry on.

"At some point after two thousand and one everyone who had a life sentence without a tariff was taken back to court and given one. His was fifteen years. He qualified for parole five years ago, but they only deemed him fit for release in the summer. I don't know whether I should have been notified about it or not. Nick said there was some sort of scheme I should have joined if I had wanted to be kept informed. I had washed my hands of him and I thought he would be in jail till the day he died."

He gets up off the bed and pulls a pair of pyjama bottoms from the drawer. He dumps the towel in the laundry basket and pulls on the trousers. He sits back on the bed across from me.

"So, has Nick been keeping tabs on him, like a private detective or something?" I ask, trying to keep my voice as upbeat as possible.

"Yes he has. The email I got from him in the early hours of Sunday morning was a shock to say the least. Nick said he had very urgent news and that I needed to phone him as soon as possible. I don't think he meant at half four in the morning and his wife was certainly not happy with me." He smiles. It is only a small facial movement, but it is most definitely a smile.

"I owe the poor guy a drink for the ear bashing he took. Anyway, he told me that he had found out Colin, that's that fucker's name by the way, was to be released again because the police had evidence that made it clear he didn't send that letter to Cheryl. The fucking stupid bitch sent it to herself because she wanted to try and make me feel sorry for her and give her money."

He shakes his head.

"I let my guard down, I believed her. They had a handwriting expert take a sample of his writing and compared it to the letter. Nothing was the same."

"That's when they tested Cheryl then?" I ask.

"Yes. She apparently denied it all at first, then tried to say it was me that had done it to scare her. She eventually owned up when they took her handwriting and compared it with the letter. She was arrested on Friday and went to court yesterday. The Sheriff remanded her in prison until after Christmas. She has been charged with wasting police time, so she will probably get slapped with a thirty-day sentence or something. I'm pursuing a restraining order on her. I want nothing else to do with her. After everything I did to help her. She's so fucked up I doubt she even cares."

He stands up and goes in to the bathroom, emerging

with the bottle of whisky. Taking a huge gulp, he sits back down.

"So what happened to your face?" My voice is quiet and I fear what he might have to say.

"This is a warning apparently."

My eyes widen in shock. "A warning for what?"

"A huge bruiser of a guy came to my office this afternoon while you were up seeing Nate. He was built like a bear. He barged right in and when I stood up to confront him, he hooked me right in the face. Now I can fight but there was no way I was even going to try with this man mountain. He could have easily killed me with a stronger punch."

I realise I'm staring at him with my jaw almost on my lap. The feelings running around in my head are a mixture of fear and love and relief. It is hard to get a grip on any one thing right now.

"What did he say to you?"

"He told me this was a warning from Colin, that he was not finished with me and never would be until the day I died."

"Steven you need to go to the police with this."

"No. I can't."

"Why? He needs to be stopped Steven."

"They can't prove he sent the guy and there was...." He looks down at the bottle in his hands. "He said if I went to the police, he would make sure you would suffer."

Oh God I can feel bile rise in my throat. I feel light headed. This is how he will get to Steven, by using his love for me. That bastard has ruined his life enough, I can't sit back and watch him do it again.

"There must be something we can do Steven. He can't treat you like this, you were a kid when all that happened." Scorching hot tears make their way down my cheeks as I speak and my words are not coherent anymore.

Steven grabs my upper arms and gives me a shake. "Gina please. He will hurt you, I know he will. It is taking a lot of self-control not to go and find the fucker and kill him. I love you Gina. I have never loved anyone like this before, ever. Every time I see you or hear your voice or even think about you my heart feels like it wants to burst right out of my chest."

He loosens his grip on my arms slightly and pulls me to him. "Gina I would die before I would ever let anything happen to you. I can't lose you, I've only just found you."

I lean back from him slightly and put my hand up to caress his face. His eyes are glassy.

"What can we do? How do we stay safe if we don't know what he'll do next?"

"Nick is giving me some extra security and he's working overtime watching Colin. One step out of line and we can get him locked back up."

"Are you saying he is already out of prison?"

"Yes he was released yesterday morning. I don't think he will come up to Scotland, not yet anyway. He obviously has scumbags that will do his dirty work for him. Nick is going to be monitoring emails and phone calls as far as he can but, in the meantime, we need to be careful. Don't go anywhere on your own or without letting your bodyguard know."

I hold my hand up and stop him. "Bodyguard? Are you kidding me? I'm not a fucking celebrity."

He looks at me a little angrily. "No, I damn well am not kidding Gina. You don't understand how dangerous that man is. He has been rotting in prison for the last twenty years. I get why he is so fucked up and hates me so much. He was landed with me when I was a baby which ruined his marriage and turned him to drink. He had to move to London to work, that meant leaving his life in Glasgow behind. There would have been no dead hooker if it wasn't for me so of course he is going to have a vendetta against me."

"Steven you need to stop blaming yourself for his actions. No one forced him to have an affair with your mum. He is the one who set all this in motion, not you."

"I know that. Gina, I have had therapy till it is coming out of my ears about this. I don't blame myself anymore, I told you that already. I'm trying to get you

87

to understand how he has processed all this. Obviously he's not going to blame himself, so I'm the next best thing. Please trust me to look after you and believe me when I say he will hurt you. Nick is working hard to dig up anything that will send him back to prison but until then we need to be careful. Will you please just do as I ask and stop being stubborn?"

I can see the worry in his eyes and I know he is making sense. "Okay."

"Good. Nick is coming by tomorrow morning. My detail will be with us when we are together and you will have your own one for when we are apart. There is going to be someone at the building tonight and when Nick gets here tomorrow, they will be relieved and our own personal guards will take over."

My mind is a mess. I'm trying my best to take all this in, but it sounds so out of this world. All this talk of security details and bodyguards has my imagination running wild.

"Okay then. Is there anything else you need to tell me?"

"Yes." He leans his head in close to me and whispers. "I love you Georgina Connor." He kisses my lips softly.

"I love you too Steven, but you have just reminded me of something I need to tell you."

He looks confused. "Okay, fire away," he says

cocking his head to the side.

"I am changing my last name back to Harper. Having his name is like a noose round my neck and I want to get rid of it. I will never forgive him for what he did to me and signing his name everywhere I go means he still has a hold over me."

Steven smiles at me. "I'm proud of you Gina you know that? You are such a strong woman. A lot of people would have given up after everything you've been through. You don't give yourself enough credit."

He stands up from the bed and lifts me into his arms. "Don't ever change," he whispers as he takes us downstairs. I kiss his cheek and snuggle in to his neck.

CHAPTER 10

NICK BRENNAN IS NOTHING like I imagined, in looks or personality. He is a little taller than Steven and is built like a weightlifter. His hair is shaved to about five millimetres all over and he has tattoos covering one whole forearm. Not a guy you would want to get on the wrong side of. However, he is surprisingly well spoken and polite. His voice is reassuring and the way he talks about his job shows how much passion and dedication he has for his trade.

"Right let's get down to business then folks," says Nick as he sits on the sofa across from us.

"Your bodyguards will be here shortly so that you can meet them and get familiar with them. I have no new leads on Colin yet, but I have managed to track down the guy who came to see you yesterday Steven. Well done on your building's security. I managed to get a good look at his face from the cameras. He's one of those guys who hires himself out to put the frighteners up people but he's a sandwich sort of a picnic when it comes to staying anonymous. We have his name and he will be locked up by now."

I stare at Nick, wide eyed. Did he go to the police about this? Steven was told I would be harmed if he did. I squeeze Steven's hand and he turns to me.

"Hey what's wrong?" He says, his eyes searching mine.

"Didn't that guy say something would happen to me if you went to the police?" I can feel the tremors in my voice and I'm trying my hardest to keep it together here.

"Oh, I'm sorry Gina," Nick says shaking his head. "No. We didn't go to the police about his threats to Steven. He has been arrested on an assault charge. You see, I have a few people on my books who will start a fight with themselves so all we did was get one of them to provoke him in a pub. I have to say the guy is a loose cannon, it really didn't take much. The pub was crowded so there were plenty of witnesses. Don't worry about him, he was actually out of prison on an electronic tag so he shouldn't have been anywhere near a pub in the first place and certainly not after seven at night. He was arrested straight away and will probably be enjoying his breakfast up at Barlinnie prison as we

91

speak."

"Thanks Nick," I say quietly. I'm startled by the buzz of the intercom.

"That will be Peter and Sarah," says Nick as Steven gets up to answer the door.

"You okay Gina?" Nick asks.

"Yes, I'm just a little bit rattled if I'm honest. I really thought things were getting better for us and then this shit has to happen. Did you ever think the universe was against you? I trust Steven and I can see you are good at your job, but it doesn't stop me from worrying."

He gives me a sympathetic smile.

"Gina, I have dealt with some crackpots in my time so believe me when I say this guy is a pussy cat compared to them. He can threaten all he likes but we will always try to be one step ahead of him."

"Thanks Nick. You're a good man." I look over his shoulder at the door as Steven walks back in followed by a tall blonde woman with scraped back hair and dressed in black. The guy is a little taller than her and built much like Nick, but he has a sterner face. He is definitely older judging by the greying at his sideburns.

"Hey guys."

Says Nick.

"You've met Steven, and this is Gina."

I stand and shake hands with them both and they

take a seat next to Nick.

"Right. This is Sarah Lowe. She will be your detail Gina. She was in the army for six years and has two tours in Afghanistan under her belt. She was also a self-defence instructor for two years."

Wow! Her credentials are amazing.

"Nice to meet you Gina," says Sarah.

"And you Sarah, thanks for this."

"It's my job, he pays us well," she says nodding to Nick.

"Steven, you've already met these guys. This is Peter Morris, Gina. He has fifteen years' experience working in the security business. Before he came to work for me was personal security for many celebrities and dignitaries. He knows his stuff. When you are going out alone Sarah will be with you and when you and Steven are together Peter will be your detail. Your phone will be programmed with their numbers and we will also have a tracking app put on it too. We will need to know where you are at all times."

I can't say anything. It feels like a total invasion of privacy. I know this is necessary until they can get that scumbag locked away again but it does not sit easily with me.

"Nice to meet you Gina," says Peter. "We are very discreet. Most of the time you won't even know we are there with you and we'll do everything we can to keep you safe."

"Thanks," I say. It's all I can say really. I can't get my head round how quickly this has all escalated. It's Christmas Eve for goodness sake. I should be looking forward to spending time with my family and giving Steven a nice Christmas not constantly looking over my shoulder or being followed by a bloody bodyguard.

"Okay Gina if you can give me your phone, I'll get everything programmed in and we will be good to go."

I pull my phone from my pocket and unlock it before I hand it to Nick. He takes it and walks to the kitchen. Sarah and Peter follow him. Steven takes my hand and pulls it up to his mouth, kissing my knuckles.

"Are you okay?" He asks, his voice low.

"I'm fine. This is all moving so quickly I feel like I'm going to get whiplash."

"I know but as soon as Nick is gone, we'll need to get on with our daily lives as if nothing has happened. Fear feeds evil and if that man thinks we have a weakness he'll try to exploit it. He will slip up, he's not that clever."

Yeah you hope. I think to myself with a half-smile on my face. I really hope he is right. I don't think my nerves will take much more drama.

Steven stands and bends to kiss my head. "I'm going to deal with some paperwork. Tell nick he can find me upstairs when he's done."

I watch him leave the living room, his body language speaking volumes and telling me what I already suspected. Steven doesn't really believe his own words. No one knows what Colin will do next and I know he is worried and having no control of the situation is probably magnifying his frustrations.

Nick returns from the kitchen with my phone and no sooner is it in my hand than it pings with a message. "I'll leave you to it. I'll be out of your hair shortly," he says with a smile as he returns to his employees in the kitchen.

Giving him my most convincing smile, I check my phone.

Hi honey what are your plans for Christmas?

It's from mum. I have an idea but I'm not sure how it will go when I suggest it to Steven.

I'll get back to you. X

I go in search of Steven. I find him tapping away at his laptop.

"Hey what you up to?" I ask.

"I'm shutting up shop for a few days," he says and looks up at me. "I've never closed my business for Christmas before." His voice is quieter than usual and I get the feeling that he is unsure about all this Christmas fuss.

"That's great because I have something to ask you."

"Okay fire away."

"Would you like to come to my parent's house with me this afternoon and stay for Christmas dinner tomorrow?"

He looks conflicted. I can see his emotions warring with each other behind his eyes. He thinks he can hide his feelings behind his mask, but the eyes don't lie. I know this is a big thing for him.

"Would your mum and dad be okay with an extra mouth to feed?"

Now, I could tell him he wouldn't be an extra mouth to feed. They always had me plus one for a long time.

"Steven, my parents think the sun shines out of your arse. Of course they won't mind. In fact, I think if you went on your own, they wouldn't even care if I was there or not."

I smile at him and he returns it. It's a genuine smile too, not forced.

"Okay then, I'll be there." He returns his gaze to the laptop and as I turn to leave, I am sure I hear him say under his breath, "I'll go anywhere with you."

I don't let on that I heard it, but it makes my heart flutter. I send a text back to mum.

We'll be over at seven and Steven is staying for Christmas dinner tomorrow. Xx

I head for the bedroom to get ready with a huge smile on my face.

CHAPTER 11

THE DRIVE TO MY parent's house is tense to say the least. We are in a Range Rover, not the Aston. Nick said this was how things had to be done to ensure no one could follow us. It was like a scene from a James Bond film. We took the Aston to the office and then took two separate taxis to a hotel in the city centre where we picked up the Range Rover in the hotel's underground car park.

Peter is following us in his car. I feel terrible that he has to spend his Christmas Eve looking after us.

Steven has uttered about four words since we picked up the car and even then it is only one-word answers to my questions. I know something is eating at him and I'm scared to ask in case I upset him. But hell, his silence is doing my head in.

"Have I done something wrong Steven?" I ask,

trying hard to keep my voice steady. No answer.

"Steven?"

Still he doesn't acknowledge me.

"God damn it Steven will you please talk to me?"

I am getting bloody angry with him now. He brings the car to a screeching halt by the side of the road. I see Peter stop his car a little way back. I turn my head to look at Steven who is still looking straight ahead.

"What's wrong Steven? Is it all this undercover shit? Are you worried about something?"

He shakes his head and looks at me. He is worried I can see it.

"Tell me what's wrong please."

He sighs. "I'm nervous okay Gina."

"About what?"

"This. Tonight. Spending Christmas day with you and your family."

I feel my forehead knit into a frown. "What do you mean? You know my dad really well and you've met my mum. You've stayed at their house before so what's different about this?"

"How do you do that Gina?"

"Do what?"

"See the positive side of everything, the good side of everything."

"Oh come on Steven, I don't see the positive side of everything. I was trying to cheer you up. Now will you tell me what is really going on in here?" I tap his head with my index finger. "Before Peter comes to find out what is going on."

He averts his gaze from me. "I've never had a Christmas before Gina. Not a proper family one. Every Christmas I had before my dad got jailed was just another day. Even when we lived with his mother."

He turns to look at me now and I can see the sadness in his eyes. "She hated me and I never had any presents to open. I asked her once when I was about six why Santa didn't visit me, and she told me Santa doesn't visit 'bastard children'. The woman was vile. It's easy to see how she spawned that piece of shit."

"Steven I'm so sorry."

"Why are you sorry? It's a part of my life I would rather forget but I can't because it is a part of my life. It is a part of what has made me who I am. I was in six different children's homes all over the country by the time I was sixteen and I can't even remember how many foster homes I ran away from. They try to make Christmas in a residential home fun, but it isn't. All Christmas in a home reminds you of is that you don't have a family. I spent eight years in homes and on only two Christmases were there any other kids there. All the other kids got to go home to their families. I only had whatever care worker had drawn the short straw to work Christmas day that year."

"Did you ever get presents?"

"Yes. There were always presents regardless of your family status. Usually it was all cheap crap that was broken by New Year. As soon as I was old enough to leave those places I did, and I gave Christmas a miss. When I started my business, I worked right through the holidays. It meant nothing to me."

He looks right into my eyes. "Until now that is."

I jump as Steven's phone rings over the speakers.

"It's Peter," he says pressing the little green phone icon to answer the call.

"Hi Steven, is everything okay with you two?"

"Yes, sorry Peter. We are going now okay?" Steven replies.

"No problem mate, I'm right behind you."

Steven hangs up and pulls away from the kerb. I glance at the clock and see it is only five past six, I told mum we would be there at seven.

"Hey, we are going to be quite early. Mum is going to love you even more, making her ever late daughter more punctual."

"Hey babe, I had your mum at hello." He flashes that boyish grin at me and all of a sudden the mood has lifted. I can see the more he tells me about himself the happier he seems.

"You're a cocky bastard you know that. You've got my mum twisted right round your wee finger," I laugh as I hold up my pinkie to him.

As we drive through the gates of my parent's driveway, I notice both of their cars at the top, but the house is mostly in darkness. The Christmas lights aren't even on. This is very strange for my mum, she normally has them on as soon as it is dusk.

Steven parks the car and Peter drives up next to us. We all get out and Steven and Peter start chatting about the security arrangements.

"I'm going inside Steven it's freezing out here," I say to him.

"Goodnight Peter, have a nice Christmas."

"You too Gina, I'll see you on Boxing Day." Peter says with a smile. His eyes are constantly scanning over our shoulders or to the side of us. He reminds me of an old Eagle Eyes Action Man doll I had when I was five.

I find the front door unlocked as I pull the handle down. I'm a little anxious that my mum and dad are playing a trick on us and that they are going to jump out and scare the bejesus out of me. As I walk through the door, I hear the faint sound of music. I can't tell what it is but knowing mum it will be Christmas songs. Closing the door behind me I hear Clio pad towards me. For a change she is not barking. Instead she comes to me and sits down at my feet looking up at me with her big puppy dog eyes. I lift her into my arms.

"Hey girl what you doing out here? Where's mummy and daddy huh?"

I am pretty sure the music is coming from the kitchen and I head for the door. I hear mum giggling and as I open the kitchen door, I'm greeted with a sight no child should ever see. Mum is sitting on the worktop, her dress pushed up round her waist and my dad is standing between her legs with his trousers round his ankles kissing her neck.

"Oh my God, I'm s-sorry. What the fuck..." I cover the dog's eyes. Why the hell I didn't cover my own is beyond me, some things can never be unseen. I back out of the kitchen, run for the front door and crash right in to Steven.

"Hey what's the rush babe?"

I can't answer him. I think I'm traumatised. I stand there like a fool shaking my head.

"Gina will you tell me what's going on you're starting to worry me." I can see in his eyes he is genuinely worried.

"Ehm, no it's nothing to worry about Steven I promise. Can you take Clio I need to go and pee?"

I hand the dog to him and make a run for the cloakroom toilet. I close the door and sit on the closed toilet lid. Now I am not a prude by any means, but I really did not need to see that. I'm glad that my mum and dad still... well… get it on, and that's good for

103

them but they are my parents. How am I going to be able to look them in the eye now? I have to spend two days with them after this.

"Gina are you okay?" Steven says as he knocks the door.

"I'm fine I'll be out in a minute."

Steven opens the door. Shit! I forgot to lock it. He is still holding Clio. "Are you going to tell me what is going on? You're freaking me out here Gina."

"Come in and close the door."

When the door is closed, I burst into hysterical laughter.

"Oh my God Steven I'm so sorry." I shake my head. "I think I just caught my parents in the process of having a quickie in the kitchen."

The smile that spreads across Steven's face is beautiful. It reaches right up to his eyes. "Oh shit. Are your retinas burned?"

I swat his arm. "It is so not funny Steven. That's not something a child should see their parents doing."

"Oh get a grip Gina, you're a grown woman. I think that it's cool actually that your dad can still get it up at almost sixty. It means there's hope for us all." He is laughing at me.

"Oh…you're a great help. Thanks for your sympathy."

There is movement in the hallway and Clio starts

struggling in Steven's arms trying to get down. When she hears my mum's voice she barks loudly, alerting them to the fact we are in the loo. Steven looks at me and motions with his head to the door. I suppose I need to face them some time. This is going to be awkward. We head out the door and are faced with two pairs of very guilty looking eyes. I don't think I have ever felt as sorry for my parents as I do right now. They look like a couple of kids who have been caught kissing behind the bike shed. We all stand there for ages until I can stand the awkward silence no longer.

"Right let's get this out the way okay?"

Everyone nods.

"Mum, dad sorry we were early. Obviously you weren't expecting us before seven, but please for the love of my bloody eyes, lock the damn door next time."

CHAPTER 12

MY MUM HAS GONE to town with the decorations this year. The house looks absolutely fantastic now that all the lights are on and she has a fire going in the lounge. I feel like I'm a kid again. It has been a long time since I have stayed with my family on Christmas Eve.

The embarrassing episode from earlier has been forgotten and we are all sitting in the lounge watching 'It's a Wonderful Life'. The room lights are off, the Christmas tree is twinkling and the fire is roaring. Mum and dad bought me a Fair Isle onesie and as soon as I unwrapped it, I put it on.

Steven and I are on one side of the couch and mum and dad are on the other. I have my feet in Steven's lap and he is rubbing them so softly and has been for the last twenty minutes. Every so often I chance a little look at him. He is totally engrossed in the film. It is one of my favourite Christmas films of all time. Steven has never seen it. He told me the only Christmas film he has really ever watched was Die Hard and even then it was only because it was an action film.

As the film comes to a close on those immortal words, 'Look, daddy. Teacher says, every time a bell rings, an angel gets his wings'; I swipe a little tear from my eye. Steven squeezes my foot and I look over at him. He has a little smile on his face and it makes my heart want to burst for him. I glance at the clock on the mantelpiece and notice that it is after midnight. Pulling my feet from Steven's lap I lean over close to him and whisper in his ear.

"Happy Christmas handsome."

He grabs my face and kisses me. Resting his nose against mine he whispers, "Thank you."

"Right folks we're going to go to bed now," I say to mum and dad. I'm exhausted. We haven't told them what has happened. I really don't need them worrying about me. They've been through enough drama where I am concerned. As far as they know Steven has taken up kickboxing to explain the cut and bruise on his face.

"Okay honey, I've made up your room and the guest room is ready for you Steven."

Oh no, no, no, mother dear. "No Steven will be staying in my room."

My mum eyes me with that look she used to give me when I was teenager. It says, 'don't push your luck young lady'. "Oh, is that right? And remind me again whose house this is?"

"Come on Carla, they are practically living together right now anyway." That's my dad, ever the peacemaker.

"No, I don't think I'm very happy about that Martin." She shakes her head.

"Mum, I wasn't going to say anything but after what I witnessed tonight, I don't think you've got a leg to stand on," I laugh at her mock shock expression and realise she has been having me on. She throws a cushion at me.

"Get to bed or Santa won't come."

I lean over the back of the couch and give both her and my dad a kiss goodnight. Steven is quiet beside me.

Mum stands up and comes around to him. She gives him a hug and a kiss on the cheek, and I hear her whisper to him, "Thank you for making my girl happy again son."

He doesn't say anything. He is overwhelmed. I need to get him out of here.

"Right goodnight guys we'll see you in the morning." I take Steven's hand and lead him out of the living room.

"Night Mr and Mrs Harper," he says as we leave the room.

As soon as we are through the door of my bedroom Steven pins me against the door and kisses me with such urgency that my lips feel bruised. When he releases me, I reach up and caress his face. The dull light from the bedside lamp illuminates his handsome face.

"Are you okay?" I ask.

"Yes, I'm fine. This has been one hell of a day hasn't it?"

"You don't say. I'll never be able to eat at that breakfast bar with a straight face again you know."

He laughs a lovely deep hearty laugh. He pushes both hands into my hair and kisses me again, this time softer. One of his hands travels down to the zip of my onesie and slides it down achingly slowly. I am anticipating his reaction when he gets the zip right down because I'm naked underneath.

He takes a breath through his teeth. "Oh fucking hell Gina," he says as he turns us and pushes me back from him.

"Do you have any idea how beautiful you are Gina Harper?"

It sounds funny being called that again, but it feels nice to know that I'm finally freeing myself of my scumbag husband.

Steven pulls the top of my onesie over my shoulders fully exposing my breasts. He grabs one of them and kneads it over and over, pinching my nipple between his fingers. By the time he puts his mouth on my nipple my senses are so heightened that it makes me jump. I can feel my heart thumping in my chest and I know it is arousal mixed with adrenaline.

He moves me backwards until I'm almost at the bed and stops me before I hit it. He eases the garment down my legs and I step out of it. I'm completely naked and feel very exposed. I move my arms to try and cover myself slightly, but he grabs them before I get the chance.

"No. Don't you dare."

I put my hands by my sides and stand there awkwardly as he stares at me.

"Do you realise how beautiful you are Gina?" I shake my head. He moves closer to me and puts his hands round my waist. He moves us so that we are standing in front of the full-length mirror in the corner of the room. I know what he is going to do and I feel my body tense. He turns me round so that I'm facing the mirror and his hands leave me for a moment while he strips himself. He kicks his clothes away from his feet and moves to stand right behind me. I feel his heat radiating out all over my back. I can't look up. I keep my eyes on my feet.

"Look at yourself Gina. Look at your beautiful body." He moves my hair to the side and places his hand on my neck right under my earlobe, pushing my chin up with his index finger so that I'm forced to look in the mirror.

"Look at this beautiful neck."

He runs his hand down my neck and rests it on my arm.

"Look at your beautiful shoulders." He brings his mouth close to the side of my head and bites my earlobe. His hand travels around me skimming my clavicle, sending a wave of goose bumps cascading over my skin. He brings it down and cups my breast. My nipples are positively aching to be touched.

"Look at your amazingly beautiful tits." He pulls my arm up and puts my hand behind his neck. I close my eyes and a little moan escapes my lips.

"Open your eyes," he whispers in my ear. His hand leaves my breast and ever so tantalisingly slowly, he moves it down my belly and towards my sex. My body is on fire. Watching him do this to me is so erotic and I'm quickly starting to lose control of my senses. If he doesn't hurry up and touch me properly, I'm going to lose the power to stand up. His hand slides ever lower and his finger softly rubs against my clit. The sensation is like being electrocuted and my whole body jerks as his finger works in little circles as if he is winding a

111

coil.

"Keep your eyes open and look at this beautiful, wet, inviting pussy." His words alone would be enough to bring on an orgasm, but he goes one better and eases a finger inside me. Swirling it round and round and in and out, he hits every sweet delicious spot he can find, and I'm so close. I close my eyes and am immediately ordered to open them.

"Watch yourself as you come Gina. I want you to see how your skin glows and your beautiful body moves." He adds another finger and presses the heel of his hand against my swollen clit and I'm done for. My body writhes and jerks as I come in great heaving waves. He keeps his hand where it is and he wrings every last ounce of my orgasm from me. The whole time I keep my eyes open and watch myself fall apart in his arms. It honestly is the most intimate thing I have ever done with anyone. Ever. I feel my body go limp as my legs try to give up on me. If it weren't for my arm round his neck and his arm round my waist, I'd be lying on the floor in a heap.

"I've got you babe," he whispers in my ear.

Before I can come down too much from that high, Steven reaches down and grabs my leg, pulling it back and hooking it round his thigh. The movement tilts my pelvis up enough for him to slip inside me. His movements are slow to start with until he finds his

112

rhythm and I my balance.

When we are in sync with each other he starts to move more quickly and I hold onto him for dear life. We are both watching the mirror. Watching each other. Looking into each other's eyes. As I feel my body get ready for another onslaught I stare straight at Steven and bite my lip. He makes a guttural noise as he slows slightly then speeds up again and empties himself into me. His hand slides down and hits my clit and off my body goes like a rocket, shooting up and slowly falling back to earth again.

Steven pulls out of me and moves us backwards. He eases us down onto the bed and I have never been so grateful to get off my feet. My legs have gone completely to jelly.

I turn to face him and kiss him lightly on his lips. "Thank you," I whisper against his mouth.

"Best Christmas ever," he whispers back and as sleep takes hold of me, I feel him shift over me pulling the blanket up and over us. I fall into exhausted, sated darkness with the final thought that I am safe in his arms.

CHAPTER 13

'SILENT NIGHT, HOLY NIGHT'

I open my eyes tentatively as the music filters to my ears. As my eyes adjust to the morning light, I turn my head and look into the beautiful blue gaze staring back at me. Steven has his head propped up on his hand with a wonderfully happy smile plastered on his face.

"Morning gorgeous," he says and leans forward to kiss my forehead.

"Morning handsome," I say back as I stretch my body in all directions. Ooh my legs are tender this morning.

"How did you sleep?" I ask him, knowing his sleeping patterns I'm surprised he is still in bed beside me.

"Like a fucking log Gina. I swear I don't think I have slept for so many hours in one go in ... well I don't actually think I ever have. It's all your fault," he laughs.

"Well I don't mind getting the blame for that. Do you think the music is mum's way of waking us without actually waking us?"

"She's had it on for the last half an hour, so, yes I think you're right. I've been lying here listening to it."

His smile is so cute and I can't help myself but touch his cheek, running my thumb along his bottom lip. "You're going to have fun today. Your best Christmas ever hasn't even started yet. I need to shower. Want to join me?"

I try a wink and I think I'm getting the hang of it, but Steven's laugh says otherwise.

"You didn't need to ask I was joining you anyway," he says and abruptly gets up off the bed and lifts me, throwing me over his shoulder. I scream rather loudly and hope mum has the music on loud enough not to hear it.

"Oh my God you are such a caveman."

I shout at him.

"Yes, me man, you woman, you go for cold shower, ha ha ha." He puts on a funny voice and before I can register the cold shower part, he turns on the water and steps under the flow with me still over his shoulder.

The water is ice cold and I squeal like a little piglet.

He puts me down as the temperature starts to rise and I bat his chest. "That was so not f-funny." I'm still shivering.

"I'm sorry, come here," he says and pulls me to him. Holding me close so that both our bodies are under the warm water.

"I don't know what you've done to me Gina. Every single day since we started this relationship, I thank my lucky stars I saw you all those months ago. I've never wanted to be with anyone like this before. I never thought I had anything to give anyone."

"You have so much to give Steven. You have given me my life back, and more." I reach up and touch his face. The little cut he got from that horrible altercation on Tuesday is healing fast and the bruising has also started do die down.

"I've never been loved so I don't really know how to give it." He sounds so sad.

"Your mum loved you Steven. Even though you don't remember it, from what you've told me I can tell she did. My parents adore you and there's me. I love you."

I squeeze some shower gel onto my hand and rub it over his chest and it starts to foam. "I love how you take care of me. How you make me happy. How you make me laugh. I love what's in here." I stop my hand over his heart. "And I love what's in here." I touch his

116

head as I put shampoo in his hair and lather it up. "And believe me you give love perfectly well my beautiful man."

"Oh Gina." He breathes out and plants his lips on mine. When he lets go, he motions with his finger to turn around. I do, and he washes my hair. First with shampoo, lathering it up and massaging my scalp, then conditioner. He pulls his fingers through my hair right to the ends smoothing out all the tangles as he goes.

"Don't get too good at that or I'll be calling on your services every time I wash my hair."

"You know I don't need an excuse to shower with you gorgeous. I think we should get washed off and go down for breakfast, I'm pretty sure I smelled cinnamon right before you woke up."

"Eee," I squeal and clap my hands like I'm five. "Cinnamon pancakes."

***

The smells coming from the kitchen have me almost drooling and as I push open the door, I'm transported back to my childhood Christmases. The morning spent having breakfast of pancakes and bacon and opening pressies. The afternoon spent building and playing with the new toys and early evening seeing how much food it is humanly possible to consume in one sitting. We walk in to the kitchen and mum turns from the hob with a huge smile on her face.

"Oh good morning you two, Happy Christmas."
She comes over and hugs us both. "I have cinnamon
pancakes and maple bacon. Take a seat and I'll get the
coffee out."

"Smells wonderful Mrs Harper," Steven says
winking at her. She turns away twittering like a little
girl and I look at him and roll my eyes.

"Oh Steven call me Carla, please," she says. She
brings our coffees to us as we take our seats at the
breakfast bar.

"Thanks Carla." He is a total charmer and I love
how this seems so normal.

Mum puts our plates down in front of us and heads
out of the kitchen to find my dad. Clio, who is
unusually subdued this morning, totters out after her.
Steven and I eat in a comfortable silence and every
now and then his knuckles brush mine between our
plates. At one point he links our pinkies and leans over
and kisses my cheek. It's like we are teenagers on a
first date, awkwardly testing the water. I understand
what is happening now when he does these little things.
It seems as though he is sometimes unsure of himself
when it comes to us being together in a non-sexual
way. Because my God he knows how to work my
body, but little things seem to be harder for him and
sometimes they appear forced or awkward.

"Are you okay handsome?" I ask taking his hand properly in mine. He looks right in to my eyes. I see a hint of tears in his. It breaks my heart to see him like this.

"I'm fine gorgeous. I'm..." he hesitates as if what he is trying to say is stuck in his throat. He shakes his head and closes his eyes sending a lone tear falling from his eye. "I'm happy Gina," he whispers, his eyes still closed.

I jump down from my stool and turn his so that I can stand between his legs. Wrapping my arms round his neck I move up onto my tiptoes and kiss his cheek then whisper in his ear. "I know, so am I."

I lay my head on his chest and he rests his chin on the top of my head. We stay like that until dad walks into the kitchen. "Is there some sort of love gas escaping from somewhere in this kitchen?" His voice booms from behind us. "I'm making up a sign for the door that says the Love Shack."

"Oh my God, dad, you're so embarrassing," I laugh at him putting on my best teenage pout.

"Are you two finished your breakfast? Mum is getting her knickers in a twist waiting to open the presents. You know how she gets about the festive season," he says with a roll of his eyes.

"I am. You ready?" I say looking up at Steven.

"Yes, let's go," he says with an unsure smile on his

face.

***

The floor under the Christmas tree is strewn with presents of all different shapes and sizes. It looks like Santa's sack threw up. Beside me Steven squeezes my hand as we assess the scene in front of us. I put my other hand over his.

"You okay?" I ask. He nods and we make our way in.

Mum is positively in her element. I'm surprised she hasn't dressed up like Mrs Claus. She did that one year when I was thirteen. Not good when you are going through puberty to have your mum be even more embarrassing than usual.

"Okay everyone find your presents." She sings the words as if she is announcing a game show. Steven and I go and sit on the floor next to the tree and mum and dad take the couch. I start looking through the presents and find one with Steven's name on it. I hand it to him and he hesitates for a second before taking it from me. I find one for mum and dad and then one for myself.

"Ready everyone, get stuck in," I say, and we all open our presents. Mum, dad and I rip our paper right off, but Steven carefully peels the tape off his and opens it with such care. I watch him, mesmerised at the meticulousness of his actions. The gift, from mum and dad, is a silvery blue silk tie. He lays the tie on the floor and folds up the paper putting it to the side. He has his head bowed and sits like that for a few moments. When he looks up, he has a smile on his face.

"Thank you so much Mr and Mrs Harper. Thank you for having me at your home. This is the first time I have experienced an actual family Christmas and I am so glad it is with you guys." He lowers his gaze again as if he is embarrassed. I reach out and hold his hand.

"Oh son, you don't need to thank us. We are happy you are here and even happier that you've given us back our little girl. So enough of that and call us Martin and Carla, please," says my dad.

"Now let's get the rest of these presents opened," he says with a huge smile and I instantly see Steven physically relax. Oh daddy I love you.

CHAPTER 14

I OFTEN WONDER IF everyone's goal at Christmas is the same as mine; to eat myself into a coma. I swear if I try to put anything else in my mouth, I'm going to have to be stretchered out. I have this thing where I will use the whole of December and most of January as an excuse to pig out on anything and everything I see. My war cry is 'oh go on then its Christmas'.

Mum's Christmas dinners are legendary. This is the meal I look forward to all year. She always makes enough to feed the whole street; today it's enough to feed a small country. Steven's face was an absolute picture when he and dad walked into the kitchen. I asked mum why she had made so much and she said it was because she was excited about having us here and things got a little out of hand. The conversation we had as we cooked dinner was not what I had expected but was what I needed.

***

"What do you need me to do mum?" I said as I walked in to the kitchen.

"Oh don't you worry about this I've got it in hand honey."

"Mum, dad and Steven are talking shop, my eyes were glazing over in there."

"Okay I'll save you. You do the potatoes. Yours were lovely last year."

Last year mum and dad came to my house for Christmas dinner. I stayed as positive as I could that day but had a roaring argument with Aiden over the fact that he didn't put his phone down the whole way through dinner. It was so rude. Now I know why.

"Right did you get goose fat?"

"In the fridge." She motioned over her shoulder as she basted the most humungous turkey I had ever seen. It looked like the thing may have been fed on steroids alone. I got what I needed from the fridge and busied myself with the potatoes.

"So," mum said in that voice that told me she was about to say something uncomfortable, "how are you and Steven doing?"

I laughed, glad she hadn't mentioned last night's kitchen quickie.

123

"Oh mum we are doing good. I really like him. I mean…I really like him."

"That's good because your dad..."

I held my hand up to cut her off. "Thinks the sun shines out his arse, I know."

"Ha, yes, that's what I was about to say, although not in those exact words. I'm glad honey. Dad and I are pleased that you had Steven with you when you found out about what happened with Aiden. I'm sorry for bringing it up but we still can't believe what he did. I honestly think if he had been here to answer for his actions your dad would have ended up in prison."

I stared at the part boiled potatoes in the colander. "I know mum. What bugs me most is that I never even realised. I mean what sort of wife doesn't notice something like that?"

"A trusting wife. Don't you dare think this was anything you did or could have prevented. The heart wants what it wants honey, some people are simply selfish when it comes to love."

I went to her and wrapped my arms round her. "Thank you mum. I love you and dad to the ends of the earth."

"And we love you now get on with those potatoes, we've got an hour before everything is ready." She looked at me with a blush on her cheeks and I knew what was coming. "So about last night..."

"Carla, I have got to say that was the best meal I have ever had the pleasure of eating." Steven sits back in his chair and throws his napkin on the table.

"Yes mum thank you. Thank you both for having us. Oh!" I jump a little when my phone pings and vibrates in my pocket. "Sorry," I say as I shift to take it out, careful not to move my stomach too much. I look at the screen and see Charlie's name. "Oh it's Charlie. She'll be wishing us a Happy Christmas with a sassy comment to follow it."

"Yes, she has a way with words that one."

Laughs mum.

Look what I got for Christmas OMG

The message is accompanied by a picture of her hand with a huge diamond ring on her ring finger.

"My God, Charlie and Mark got engaged today! Look," I say holding the phone up to let everyone see the picture.

"Oh my, that's lovely," mum says. "A new wee baby and a wedding to plan."

"I have to call her, excuse me." I get up from the table and go in to the lounge where it is quiet. I'm about to press the green call button when I hear the kitchen door open and Steven's voice. He must be on the phone too. I stop and listen.

125

"What's the damage Cerys? Only that one? How the fuck did he know that's where that money was? Is there anything we can do right now? I know, I know obviously this is the best time to hit a bank account. Goddamn holidays. Right this is what I want you to do. Call Nick and find out what information he has gathered, and I want both of you to meet me at the house later." He sighs and I can take the suspense of this no longer.

I get up and walk out of the lounge. Steven's eyes widen on seeing me and he shakes his head.

"What's going on?" I ask. He holds a finger up to his mouth to tell me to be quiet. I do but I'm becoming increasingly worried and I have a feeling I won't be told the whole story unless I threaten it out of him.

"Okay I'll contact Peter. I'll speak to you later. Yes, bye."

He hangs up and closes his eyes, sighing.

I put my hand on his arm and ask tentatively.

"What's happened Steven?"

"Oh Gina I wish you weren't with me right now."

The shock on my face causes him to rephrase.

"Sorry, what I mean is I wish I could sort all this shit out without you being involved. I'm trying to keep you, us, safe and I feel like I'm slowly losing control."

"Please Steven, tell me what happened."

"One of my bank accounts has been hacked and

emptied."

"Oh my God, how much was stolen?"

"There was a little over fifty thousand in it. It's not the money that's the problem though. Nick is certain it was Colin who stole the money. That money has been in my possession since I was one month old. My mother put a lump sum into a bank account for me when I was a baby and it could never be accessed by anyone but me and only when I turned twenty-one. It was half the money she inherited when her grandmother died. He knew about it and was always pissed he couldn't get access to it." Steven takes my arm and leads me in to the lounge and we sit on the couch.

"I assume you did get access to it then."

"Yes as soon as I was old enough, but I never moved it. I used some of it, I was a student so I needed it, but the rest stayed in the bank. I've never added to it so anything it is worth now is purely interest. I didn't want to touch it because it was the only thing I had left that she gave me. I'm certain it's the only reason he took me on."

"Do you think that's why he only targeted that account?" I can't believe how low this nasty man is willing to go but I have a feeling this is only the beginning.

"Yes and obviously he knew where the money was.

I wish I had moved it. I know he has only done this to scare me, but I'm worried Gina. Not for myself. I couldn't give a shit about me; it's you I need to protect. I honestly don't want you anywhere near the places he knows but I can't bear to be apart from you. Fuck!" He says as he closes his eyes and runs his hand down his face.

"I'm not going anywhere Steven. I couldn't stand it if anything happened to you. We have good security and I have confidence in Nick's abilities. They'll get him."

"I need to go Gina. I have to meet with Nick at the house. You can stay here and I can have Sarah come for you in the morning or you can come with me now. Whatever you decide please don't tell your parents."

He gets up and walks towards the door.

"I'm coming with you. I'll make up an excuse for them, you go and get ready."

I make my way to the kitchen door. I'm not really sure what I am going to tell them, but I can't let Steven go on his own. This thing has gotten very real now and I know my parents will try to stop me from going with him if they know what is going on. I take a deep breath, plaster a smile on my face and push open the door.

CHAPTER 15

STEVEN'S HOUSE IS BUZZING with activity and as I sit on the sofa in the lounge, I am left under no illusion about why he is so successful. The way he holds himself as he speaks to people and delegates with total authority and confidence is amazing to watch. I have to say I'm rather in awe of him. Peter and Sarah are both here and so is Nick. There are a couple of other people I don't recognise but I assume they are with Nick. They have spent the whole time in the kitchen on laptops. It is like a mini tech lab in there. And the phones. My God the phones are ringing off the hook. I actually cannot believe how much activity there is considering it is eight o'clock on Christmas night.

I jump as the intercom buzzes. Sarah answers it and opens the door. After a few seconds I see Gerry come through the lounge doors followed closely by the blonde vision that is Cerys. This is the first time I have met her. I have never even spoken to her and I'm slightly apprehensive. I'm taken by surprise when she drops her bag and strides right over to me. As she gets closer, I can see how absolutely stunning she is. That picture in the online article I saw did not do her justice. She grabs my hands and yanks me off the couch pulling me close and hugging me hard.

"Gina, it is so nice to finally meet you," she says, in her strong Welsh accent. She pulls back from me only enough so that she can still talk quietly. "Thank you Gina, thank you thank you thank you."

"Eh, you're welcome, but I don't know what for." I look at her with a puzzled expression.

"Oh God are you kidding? Ever since he started seeing you, he has been the best boss ever," she laughs. Funnily enough this is not the first time I have heard that.

"Okay. So, you are the famous Cerys then?"

"Sure am babe and you know something, he said you were beautiful but wow."

"Um thanks."

She reminds me of Charlie in the way she just says what she thinks. I think I'm going to get on well with her.

"I really wish we had met under better circumstances but since we are here would you like a drink?" I motion towards the kitchen.

"Oh it's okay honey I'll get it I need to go and speak to Lord Parker anyway. I'll get you one." She lifts my glass from the coffee table and walks confidently to the kitchen.

Looking around the room I try to take all this in. Why are these people not with their families? It's Christmas day for goodness sake. Today's events could rival the best British soap opera Christmas Special with the amount of drama we've had.

Gerry sits down beside me on the sofa. "You okay Gina?" He asks.

"I don't really know how I feel to be honest Gerry. It's all a bit overwhelming. Why are you not with your girlfriend or your daughter today?"

"Well Laura, my daughter, is with her mum today. I see her on Boxing Day but she is sixteen now so I don't know how much longer that is going to last. Julia, my fiancée," he winks at me, "is fine with me being here."

"Oh my God when did you get engaged?"

"Today," he says with a huge smile on his face and a twinkle in his eye.

"No way, love must be in the air, Charlie and Mark got engaged today too. Congratulations," I say and kiss him on the cheek.

"Hey, stop molesting my staff." I look up and see

Steven and Cerys standing in front of us. Cerys hands me my wine then nudges Steven in the ribs. He laughs at her. I don't understand why he is so smiley and totally unstressed looking. Grabbing my hand, he pulls me up from the sofa.

"Excuse us folks, I need to speak to Gina for a moment." He leads us out into the hallway and through the doors of the TV room. "Sit down," he says motioning to the sofa as he closes the doors behind us. He walks over to the TV and turns it on. He sits beside me with the remote control in his hand.

"Is everything okay Steven?"

"Yes, it is actually." He points the remote at the TV and the black screen comes to life. He presses a few buttons and four CCTV mini screens appear. One shows the front of this building and another shows the back. The other two show different angles of the entrance to the apartment.

"These were installed when I bought the house, but I've never had them live because I didn't feel the need before..." he looks right into my eyes, "before you."

"Did you never want to keep yourself safe?"

"I didn't care about myself Gina, I didn't care about anyone. The only thing I ever gave a shit about was proving wrong anyone who ever doubted me. Anyone who said I would never be anything, never make anything of my life because I was worthless."

"Is that what he used to say to you? Are you trying to prove him wrong?" I ask as I softly stroke his knuckles.

"Oh fucking shut up Gina. Why would I care what that fucker thinks of me?"

I feel rage boiling inside me. I let go of his hand and grab his t-shirt at the neck pushing him back slightly. I am so fucking angry with him.

"You listen to me," I say through gritted teeth as I look right into his eyes. "You have nothing to prove to anyone Steven. Regardless of how you got here or the circumstances of your life that have led up to whatever is going on now, you are a good person. You have so much to give and so many people who actually care about you so don't you dare ever speak to me like that again. I'll help you sort this shit out but you have to stop pushing me away."

I feel my body start to shake and my composure is about to take a nosedive. I feel like I'm talking to myself four or five weeks ago. Steven stares at me for the longest time before he prises my hands from his t-shirt, his lips curving ever so slightly.

"Do you know how sexy you look when you're angry?"

"Steven stop changing the subject and stop fucking laughing at me."

"Come here," he says and pulls me close to him.

133

"What's wrong?"

"I hate him Steven. I don't even know the bastard and I hate him." I take a deep breath and try to calm myself. "He tried to ruin your life when you were a child and he's trying to do it again. I want to believe that Nick can handle this and that you, we, will be okay but I'm scared. I can't lose you Steven."

"Oh Gina I'm so sorry," Steven whispers against my hair.

"Please stop pushing me away Steven. I want to help you." I sit back and look into his eyes.

"You were right." His voice is so quiet.

"I know."

"He always told me I was a worthless piece of shit, that I was looking at my future when I looked at him. That used to scare me and it still does Gina. What if I do end up like him? What if your genes determine more than your eye or hair colour or whether or not you can roll your tongue? I don't want to be like him."

"Hey, you are nothing like him and you bloody well know it. You are a good person Steven. You care about other people for a start, so you are already better than him."

He shrugs. "Listen," he says moving closer to me on the couch. "We don't need to hide from this Gina. Nick is good at what he does, he has everything covered so we need to appear as normal as we can."

"It will be hard to do that with all this in the back of our minds, but I think you are right."

"I have something planned for New Year. I'm not telling you what it is but trust me you'll love it," Steven says as he stands and takes my hand, pulling me up from the sofa and kissing me softly. "Come on let's go and see what's been happening out there. I want everyone out so that I can have you to myself for a while."

He leads me out the door and back into the thick of the action with the intrigue of New Year buzzing in my mind.

CHAPTER 16

I LOVE GOING ON a trip, but I really like to know where I am going first. Steven has been very cryptic since Christmas day, only giving me obscure hints. He said where we're going was his idea of paradise, where the sand is white and the sea is blue-green. This conjured up visions of the Caribbean, palm trees and bikinis. However, I am now standing on the tarmac at Glasgow Airport looking at a tiny Cessna aircraft thinking that might not be what Steven has in mind.

"So are you going to tell me where we are going yet?" I ask looking at the side of his face. His mouth curls in a smile.

"Nope."

"You know this really isn't fair. I couldn't even pack my own bag because I don't know where we are going."

"I know I love watching you squirm. The suspense is killing you isn't it?"

"Oh, so observant." The sarcasm is dripping from my voice. I give him the evil eye and he laughs as a man in a smart pilot suit approaches us.

"Mr Parker, Ms Harper." He nods to us and shakes Steven's hand, then mine.

"My name is Robert Simpson, but you can call me Bob, I will be your pilot for today. We have perfect flying conditions so you will have a fabulous view. Melissa here will get you settled and we will be ready for take-off in around twenty minutes." He nods towards the tall redhead on his left.

I can't help but smile. I have flown plenty of times on large commercial aeroplanes but never on a private plane. I am so excited I want to burst but I don't want to appear like a child. I can't wait to tell Charlie about this.

"Good morning," says Melissa. "Come this way and we will get you seated and relaxed before take-off."

We follow her to the steps of the aircraft her slim body moving gracefully in her perfect navy-blue uniform. As we enter the inside of the plane I gasp. There are eight seats, two rows of four facing each other, clad in cream leather. From the wood trims to the plush cream carpet, this is pure luxury.

"Take a seat anywhere you please. Can I get you both a drink?" Melissa asks us both but really only acknowledges Steven with her eyes.

"Champagne and Strawberries please Melissa," Steven replies.

"Very good sir," she says as she saunters off leaving us to take our seats.

When she is out of earshot I wink at Steven. "She likes you."

"What can I say, I have that effect on the ladies." He winks back at me and it makes me giggle.

We stow our bags and take our seats, facing each other.

"So are you going to tell me where we are going? I honestly can't take the suspense any longer. This is so cruel."

"Of course I'm not going to tell you, I'm enjoying this far too much. Your wee face is a picture. Don't worry you'll find out soon enough. I've arranged a light lunch for us when we are in the air. The flight will only take about an hour."

"Okay, I'll let it go for now, but you owe me boyo."

I turn and take a look out the small window next to me. It is such a beautiful day. The winter sun is low in the crystal-clear blue sky. I look over at Steven, who is reading something on his phone, and smile. Perfection, that's what this day is. I pull my iPad from my bag and open my Kindle app. As I open my book, Melissa comes back with our champagne. She puts the glasses down in front of us and explains that we will be served our food as soon as we are in the air. Steven reaches over and takes his glass and holds it up.

"Cheers babe." He smiles. I lift mine and we clink them together as the pilot's voice comes over the intercom to let us know that we will be on our way in five minutes. And damn it, he doesn't say where we are going.

***

The sandy beach below us seems to stretch for miles as the plane heads towards the runway. Sure enough the flight only took around an hour and the view was absolutely stunning the whole way here. I have had a bird's eye view of parts of Scotland I never even knew existed. What a stunning country I call home. I now know that we are heading for Stornoway in the Outer Hebrides off the west coast of Scotland. This flight has actually left me somewhat embarrassed. I have lived in Scotland my whole life and I don't think I have ever ventured any further north than Edinburgh. Seeing the magnificent mountains, stunning lochs and lush green woodland sprawled out beneath us has given me a real sense of appreciation for my surroundings. I feel like I am looking at my whole life the same way these days, as though a fog has lifted and everything is in vivid colour.

As the plane comes to a halt Melissa reappears and helps us with our bags. "I hope you had a nice flight with us today. I will see you on your return journey. Have a great new year."

We both thank her and Bob the pilot. We also meet his co-pilot for the first time. I didn't even know there were two of them.

A man in a smart suit and hi-vis vest shows us to the terminal and Steven chats to him about the vehicle we will have for the next few days and gives him our return details. He walks us through the terminal building and out to the car park and shakes both our hands as he leaves.

"Ready?" Steven asks.

"Oh absolutely. I sure hope you packed me some jumpers in here," I say shrugging my bag up my shoulder. Steven leans in close to my ear and whispers.

"I did but you'll not be needing them much." He moves away and winks at me and I can't help the stupid girly giggle that escapes my lips.

"Come on let's go, we still have a fifty-mile drive to get to where we are going."

Fifty miles, I feel as though we are so far removed from everywhere already. If we go any further, we may fall off the edge of Scotland. The vehicle we come to a stop in front of is a shiny black pickup truck. It is huge and imposing and I can imagine this thing will power through any adverse weather conditions we may happen to get caught in. Steven pulls a set of keys from his pocket. I didn't see anyone give him the keys. He probably owns the bloody island, so I don't ask. We dump our bags in the back seat and set off.

The drive across the Isle of Lewis and Harris is even more stunning than seeing Scotland from the air. The rugged, lunar-like terrain and wide-open space is so peaceful. It is postcard perfect with its little cottages dotted here and there, the sheep wandering over the frost covered moors and the beautiful lochs around almost every bend.

We are now on a single-track road with rocky hills and heather on either side of us, everything covered by a thin layer of white frost.

As we take a sharp turn in the road a huge expanse of water opens up before us. It is crystal clear and absolutely stunning.

"Oh," I whisper.

"Beautiful isn't it? You ain't seen nothing yet," he laughs.

I can't take my eyes from the view and as the truck approaches the brow of a little hill I gasp and hold my hand over my mouth. Ahead of us in the distance I can see a line of pure white sand and the water beside us has started to turn a beautiful blue-green colour. Paradise. My body is tingling all over as we go further up the road. One could be forgiven for forgetting that they are actually still in Scotland. This is pure unspoilt beauty.

We pass a few cottages and holiday homes but carry on further up the track until we come to a modern white and wood building. It is two stories high and there is a balcony of glass on the second floor that wraps round most of the building. It is beautiful but what I notice most as I get out of the vehicle are the steps that lead from a decked area in front of the house right down onto the beach.

"This will be home for a few days, my little slice of heaven," says Steven coming up behind me and wrapping his arms around my waist.

"Steven this is amazing. This view is…well …there are no words." It's true. There are no words that could actually do this place justice.

"Come on let's get these bags inside and then we will go for wee stroll on the beach before it gets dark." Steven looks out across the water and says with a smile, "I absolutely love this place Gina."

He gets our bags from the back of the truck and walks towards the house. I honestly don't think I have seen him look so at peace since I met him. It is really nice to see. Obviously being so far removed from the grind of daily life and all the crap that comes with it is having a good effect on him.

The inside of the house is just as modern and stylish as the outside. There is a sleek open plan kitchen and lounge that takes up the whole ground floor. The windows wrap around two whole sides giving a completely uninterrupted view of the beach and water. Sunk into the middle of the floor is a round fire and it's already lit, warming the room perfectly. Yes, by far and away this place is paradise. I am totally in love with it already and I can't wait to get my camera out and start taking pictures.

Steven has already gone upstairs with our bags, so I climb the stairs to join him. I know if downstairs is as gorgeous as this, upstairs will blow me away and I am not disappointed. The view from the master bedroom, where Steven is hanging our clothes, is even more spectacular than the one downstairs. The windows span three sides of this huge room. A wall of glass bricks sections off a third of the room. Taking a look round the wall I find a massive en-suite bathroom. A huge bath sits diagonally facing the windows. Having a soak in this tub would be like bathing in the Atlantic Ocean, although, I imagine the bath would be about forty degrees warmer. A balcony wraps right around the whole top floor of the building providing a breath-taking 360-degree view. I walk back through to the bedroom and Steven turns and smiles at me.

"Do you like it?" He asks.

"Oh my God yes Steven. This whole place is out of this world. I know this is a stupid question, but do you own this house?"

"Yes, I designed it and had it built a year and a half ago. I come up here when I want to get away from things for a while. It's so peaceful and beautiful. It really makes you appreciate life seeing all this in front of you."

He pulls a cream chunky knit jumper from the bag and tosses it to me. "Wrap up gorgeous. The Atlantic wind is mighty chilly at this time of year."

I take off my jacket and pull the jumper over my long-sleeved tee. It is super soft and cosy and fits perfectly. Steven takes off his jacket and gets a navy jumper from the bag for himself.

We head out of the house and down the steps to the beach. As we walk hand in hand along the white sand with only the sound of the waves lapping beside us, I can see why he is so happy here.

CHAPTER 17

THE WATER RUNNING OVER my arms is beautifully warm as I lie in the bath with my back against Steven's chest. He soaks the sponge and lets it run over the same place over and over. I was right. All you can see from this angle is water. The sun has dipped just below the horizon and the last glimmer of light shining up into the sky is a fiery reddish-orange, fading to vibrant pinks and lilacs. The view from here is otherworldly. Our walk on the beach was so refreshing but I was chilled to the bone. I could stay in this tub all day if left to it.

"I think we are going to need to get out of here soon gorgeous. As much as I'm loving every minute of it, we need to eat. I've had some fresh seafood delivered for dinner and if we time it right there is a surprise for afters."

"Seriously will you stop with the surprises? I can't take it anymore." I pout, even though he can't see me.

"But it's so much fun," Steven laughs moving me forward and standing up. He steps out and wraps a towel round his waist then wraps me up in a huge fluffy white bath towel as I get out. He pulls me into him and kisses my lips so softly, lingering for a second before wrapping his arms round me and hugging me close. I lay my head against his damp chest. I can feel his heart beating.

"I love you my beautiful girl," he whispers against my hair. I close my eyes and melt into him.

***

Dinner was absolutely amazing. We had a whole range of beautiful seafood dishes from Cullen Skink to scallops and langoustines. Even though I had a lot to eat I don't feel over full, the food was so light that there was definitely room for dessert. We are sitting on the floor in the living room in front of the fire eating raspberry cranachan from cute little glasses. Steven has no TV in this house. He says he likes the peace too much, so we are listening to some music. It is dark now and curtains cover the windows behind us, the only light in the room is the fire. Every now and then Steven catches my eye and smiles.

"What?"

"I'm so happy you are here with me Gina. I couldn't imagine seeing in a new year anywhere else or with anyone else." He stands up and holds out his hand to me. "Come with me, it's time for your surprise." He pulls me up from the floor and takes my empty dessert glass. He puts them in the sink and then we make our way upstairs to the bedroom. The curtains are fully drawn up here too and I wonder what on earth he has in store for me.

"Stand over there and face the wall." I do as he says, and feel him come up behind me. He puts a scarf over my eyes and blindfolds me. I'm immediately excited and apprehensive all at once. I can hear him busying himself behind me. I hear him open the curtains and when the doors onto the balcony are opened, I feel the cool air flood into the room. After a moment he is back behind me shielding me from the cold with a blanket.

"Right turn round. I'm going to walk you to the doors and out onto the balcony. Don't worry I won't let you trip up."

"This is exciting," I whisper as I turn. Steven walks me forward, making sure I lift my feet fully over the threshold of the doors. He lets go of my arm and moves behind me and I feel him start to untie the scarf.

"Ready?"

"Yes."

As the scarf drops from my eyes and I take in the sight before me, every single nerve ending in my body tingles. I'm finding it hard to process what I'm seeing. The bright green light dances across the entire sky in waves and above it there is a blanket of beautiful stars. This is the most beautiful, spectacular thing I have ever witnessed. I put my hand over my mouth and realise that the breath I inhaled when my eyes were uncovered is starting to burn my lungs.

"Oh my God," I manage to breathe out again and turn to look at Steven. Now I know why he had all the curtains closed. He has a huge smile on his face.

"Surprise," he whispers and holds out my camera. I don't take the camera; instead I throw my arm round his neck and kiss his wonderful lips.

"Thank you Steven, a million times thank you."

I let him go and take the camera. The shots I get are amazing. I have seen plenty of pictures and videos of the Northern Lights but to actually witness them in real life is beyond words. Steven takes my camera from me and takes it into the bedroom. When he comes back out, he is carrying a bundle of blankets.

"Are you cold?" I ask nodding to the blankets. He doesn't answer me. Instead he walks to the corner of the balcony where there is a huge cube draped with a weather cover. He pulls the cover off and underneath is a double rattan day bed. He dumps the blankets down on the bed and comes back to me.

"Get naked gorgeous," he says ushering me back into the room.

I go in and get stripped, making a detour to the bathroom to freshen up a little and head back out to the balcony with my blanket wrapped round me. As I step out onto the balcony, I find Steven lying on the bed under the blankets and a patio heater warming the air around it. I pull the doors to the bedroom closed and join him under the covers. The Aurora is still bright in the sky above and it reflects off the water below. He pulls me in close and claims my mouth in a deep passionate kiss, our tongues doing a dance that could rival the lights in the sky.

"You are so beautiful Gina," Steven says as he trails his hand down my face, then my neck and it disappears under the covers. He lightly runs his fingers over my nipple and carries on down until he is stroking my sex. My hips buck under his touch, my eyes closing automatically, though I wish they wouldn't. He plays his fingers over me with the lightest of touches. It sends sensations all over my sensitised skin and then he eases a finger inside me and rubs his thumb over my clit. I grab at the blankets desperate for something to hold on to. It takes no time at all for him to get me to orgasm and as my body responds he catches my moans with his kiss. When he lets my mouth go, I open my eyes and notice that the lights are starting to fade leaving behind a completely clear sky.

"Look at the stars Steven," I whisper.

"Let's look at them together," he says, and he moves up the bed so that his torso is leaning against the cushions on the back. He grabs my waist and pulls me up and onto his lap, my legs bent under me on either side of his hips. I can feel his hard-on against my back. He places kisses on my back as he lifts me and brings me down onto him, both of us moaning in sheer delight as he slides right in to the hilt. I lay my back against his chest and as I move up and down his hands are on my breasts, his fingers tweaking my nipples. We are barely covered by the blankets and the cold air should be chilling me, but my body is on fire and we move in unison, both of us mesmerised by the spectacular night sky. Resting my head on his shoulder, we both look up at the stars. I feel as though I'm hurtling towards them and I can do nothing to stop it. I try to hold myself back as long as I can, but it is no use especially when I feel Steven thicken inside me.

"Let it go Gina," he says through gritted teeth and brings one of his hands down to rub my clit. I can hold out no longer and as I come in great waves, I keep my eyes on the stars above. It is heavenly. I feel as though we are welded together like some celestial being, rising up into the night sky. I have never experienced anything like this before. Steven's movements still slightly, then speed up again and I know he is right there with me.

"Oh fuck Gina." He pours himself into me as we both look up at the stars and start to come down from our high.

I can only hear the water lapping at the shore below us and our ragged breathing. Steven lifts me onto the bed beside him, pulling the blankets up over us. The immediate heat against my cool skin is welcoming and almost at once I feel my limbs become heavy. He props himself up on one elbow and strokes the side of my face.

"Do you have any idea how beautiful you are, out here among all these stars? You belong up there with them." He kisses me softly and my eyes close as I feel myself drift off, the stars seeming to fizz out one by one behind my eyelids until there is nothing but darkness.

***

My hair blowing over my face wakes me with a start. Looking up and seeing the beautiful night sky above me I realise we are still outside, although I am not cold. The heater is still giving off a nice warm glow. I'm in Steven's arms and his body heat is cocooning me. His breathing is deep and even. He is sound asleep. I wonder how long we have been out here. I think it was about eight pm when we came outside. I hope we haven't missed midnight. I really want to see in the New Year conscious. Leaning up, I try to look at Steven's watch, but my elbow slips out from under me. I bump back down again, rousing Steven from his slumber.

"Hey you okay?" He says, his voice laden with sleep.

"I'm fine sorry I was trying to see the time and I slipped."

He looks at his watch. "It's only eleven forty, we're early," he laughs and stretches out his body. "I could get very used to this sleeping thing you know. I've slept more beside you in the last month than I have in forever. Come on let's get some drinks to see in the New Year. "

"Can we bring them out here? I can't get enough of this." I gesture up to the sky.

"Yeah it is something special isn't it? Wait here," Steven says as he kisses me on the head and gets off the bed giving me an uninterrupted view of that gorgeous toned arse of his.

When he disappears through the doors I lie back and pull the covers up over me, staring at the sky. I can pick out a few of the well-known constellations from my limited knowledge but I'm amazed at how many

152

stars I can actually see. Up here there is very little, if any, light pollution so the eyes can see things that the bright lights of the city drown out. I have to admit, I feel rather insignificant looking at this.

"Penny for them?" I'm startled out of my little melancholic dream and see Steven standing next to the bed with two champagne flutes in one hand and a bottle of Cristal in the other. And damn it, he has put on a pair of trousers.

"I was lying here looking at the stars feeling a bit insignificant. It's hard to get your head around how much is out there. I mean we'll never really know, will we? Not in our lifetime anyway."

"Jesus Gina you were smiling when I left you." He pours me a glass of bubbly and hands it to me. "Get this down you and get that beautiful smile back on your face."

I take the glass from him and watch as he pours himself one, the little bubbles rising like drops of gold.

"It's five to midnight. Nearly time to say goodbye to this very eventful year."

"Yeah good riddance to it. The only good thing this year brought me was you."

Steven leans in and kisses me, his lips lingering a moment.

"I want all your new years from now on Gina."

That's a bold statement. I know deep down in my

heart that this is what I want too, but I can't seem to admit it, not yet, and I don't know how to respond.

"I know you do but can we just focus on getting this one under our belts and see where things go from there?"

He looks a little dejected and I immediately feel bad. Obviously sensing this from the look on my face, he smiles and says, "Let's get these glasses charged."

We sit in silence as we wait for the turn of the year. As the hands of Stevens watch move towards the number twelve it feels as though they are wiping out all the nastiness of this year but what is heading our way in the next?

"Happy new year gorgeous," Steven whispers in my ear.

"Happy new year handsome. Onwards and upwards babe." We clink our glasses together and settle back to look at the stars, a universe of possibilities before us.

CHAPTER 18

"YOU LUCKY BITCH GINA," Charlie coos. She is sitting beside me on the sofa in Steven's TV room looking at my photos from our trip. It's the first I have seen her since before Christmas.

My new camera is fabulous and well worth the extortionate amount I paid for it. We had three days in blissful paradise and Steven was right about not needing many clothes, we spent most of the time in bed or at least wrapped up in blankets wherever we happened to be in the house. It was a good enough excuse since it rained until we were due to leave.

We have been back for five days now and things seem to be going okay. I have gotten used to being followed everywhere. Nothing has been heard of Colin and as far as we know he is attending his parole appointments in London. Obviously he has people to carry out his vendetta for him so we can't be complacent but right now there is an air of calm around us and I'm going to bask in it.

"Yeah, I am a little bit lucky, aren't I? I swear Charlie I have never seen anything so beautiful in my life. These photos are good but there is nothing I can say that can describe it."

"Stop rubbing it in woman. You've already made me jealous with the private plane and the house and the beach. Next you'll be telling me *'oh we made love under the stars'*." She says in a mockingly lovey tone and smiles as she looks at me. I feel my cheeks flush. Charlie rolls her eyes.

"Oh for God sake Gina, I thought I was making a joke. Does he really have to be so damn perfect?"

"You have no idea Charlie. I still have to pinch myself now and again to believe all this is real."

"Gina if you even dare to say it's too good to be true, I am actually going to bitch slap you."

I laugh. I can always trust Charlie to tell it like it is. "Nope not this time honey. I do deserve to be happy. After everything, I deserve it and he does make me happy Charlie. I'm finally seeing everything much clearer now, I wish I could have seen it sooner."

"Well halle-fuckin-lujah," Charlie says and stands up taking a bow as if to an imaginary audience. "I thank you ladies and gentlemen, my work here is done."

"Hey bighead, come and sit down and finish looking at these."

She sticks out her tongue and comes to sit down beside me.

"I hope you put the porno shots on a different card, I might go into labour if I see something I shouldn't."

"Oh God Charlie, speaking of things you shouldn't see. I caught my mum and dad in a rather compromising situation on Christmas Eve. We got there too early and they were in the throes of a quickie in the kitchen."

She snorts and then starts laughing hysterically. "Bet you were mortified you wee prude."

"Hey, I am not a prude, but, come on, that's not something you want to see your parents doing!"

"Oh Gina, Nikki and I used lie in bed at night giggling at the noises coming from our parents' bedroom. They used to be at it like rabbits. If we get to their age and are still doing stuff like that, we should think ourselves lucky."

My phone pings with a text. Saved by the bell. It is from Steven.

Hey babe, missing you. Xx

Charlie gets up from the couch shaking her head.

"Can you two not be apart for five minutes? I'm off

to the loo, want a drink on my way back?"

"Yes please, there's fresh orange in the fridge."

She walks out the door chuckling to herself. I open the text message properly and tap out a reply.

Missing you too handsome. Xx

I hit send and within seconds there is a reply.

I keep picturing you naked in front of that fire in Harris. Mmm. X

A huge smile spreads across my face. We had some fun in front of that fire. I sit back against the couch and close my eyes remembering. Remembering Steven's hands working their way slowly over my entire body. The light of the fire shimmering in his eyes, turning them from deep blue to liquid gold.

"Ooh sexting now. I was only gone five minutes. Thank God I came back when I did, who knows what I would have seen."

Charlie's voice startles me and I open my eyes to find her standing in front of me holding two glasses of orange juice. I quickly click off my messages.

"You wee creeping Jesus Charlie. I didn't even hear you come back there."

"I know, I had to speak, I was afraid you were going to start feeling yourself up. I'm all for self-satisfaction babe but I don't want to watch."

158

"Oh shut up." I try to feign indifference, but I'm failing miserably. I can feel my cheeks burning. I would love to be like Charlie, nothing seems to embarrass her. She sits back down beside me wincing a little as she does.

"Are you okay honey?"

"Yeah, I've started getting very mild Braxton Hicks contractions, but the midwife told me it's normal. I got worried over New Year because they were a bit painful. I've still got over a month to go and the midwife I saw told me that the real ones will be much more painful so I'm in the process of changing my birth plan to get as many drugs as is possibly legal."

"Well I could sit here and say it won't be that bad, but I've watched those shows with women giving birth and I'm sorry, but it does look like it's going to bloody hurt."

She looks at me with a pout. "Thanks for the support."

"Hey, you're rubbing off on me. I'm just telling it like it is."

Charlie punches me on the arm as my phone sings a happy little tune telling me I have an appointment.

"I have to go and sign my paperwork for the new house. Why don't you come with me and we can go and do some shopping and get an early dinner before you have to go home?"

159

"You had me at shopping babe, let's go."

There is a definite bite in the air as we step out of the front door. The solicitor's office is only a five-minute drive away in the city centre so we head out to the main road to hail a taxi. As we walk, I hear the sound of a car engine not too far behind us. Sarah is hot on our tail. I know the drill by now. I have to text her with my destination address before I go anywhere. She drives a different car and changes her appearance every day. I know Colin is dangerous, but I feel as though this is a tad over the top. Luckily we get a cab straight away.

"How you coping with all this MI5 stuff?" Charlie asks as we settle in the back and watch as Sarah drives off ahead of us.

"You know it's not really that intrusive, Sarah is very discreet and sometimes it means I have someone else to talk to through the day which is nice. I just want all this to be over Charlie. It's been one thing after another since I first met Steven."

She puts her hand on mine. "He's a good guy honey and I'm glad he's keeping you safe. I'm sure things will be back to normal soon enough. Now where are we going shopping?"

"I haven't a clue, let's see where our feet take us." I smile at her as the taxi stops outside the solicitor's office.

I pay the driver and we get out onto the pavement. I can see Sarah's car idling by the kerb. She is driving a nice little sporty looking Mercedes today. Yesterday she was in a little Fiat 500 puddle jumper. My phone pings with a text. It's from Charlie. I look at her with a puzzled expression.

Let's ditch the bodyguard for the afternoon.

I tap a reply.

I can't. Steven would have a shit fit.

I watch as she types her own reply.

Bummer. ☹

"Come on you'll not even know she's here," I reassure her as we head in to the building.

The signing of the paperwork took all of ten minutes. I now officially have my very own home. Charlie and I are now in Frasers happily misting ourselves with enough perfume testers to put a hole in the ozone layer. The shop is absolutely heaving with January Sales bargain shoppers.

I'm about to turn to Charlie with a bottle of the new Marc Jacobs perfume when I'm barged from behind and go tumbling to the floor. The perfume bottle smashes under my hand and my phone takes a slide right across the floor. I sit down next to the counter and look at my hand, which is bleeding quite badly, the little shards of glass glinting in the lights of the perfume counters.

"Oh my God Gina are you okay?" Charlie kneels down on the floor beside me as a crowd forms round us.

"I didn't know perfume bottles could smash like that." I hear a woman say. I'm a little shocked at the blood pouring from my hand, but I can't take my eyes off it.

"I've called an ambulance honey, they've told me to ask you to hold your arm higher up than your heart to try and stop the blood flow until the paramedics get here." Charlie pulls my hand up as I lean back against the glass cabinet.

"Where is my phone Charlie?"

"Fuck the phone just now Gina, you're bleeding here."

"I need to call..." I'm about to say I need to phone Sarah when she appears from the crowd with my phone in her hand. She must have been tailing us in the store. She's bloody good, I didn't even see her.

"If the ambulance doesn't get here in the next five minutes, I'm taking you up to the hospital myself," Sarah says, constantly looking anywhere but at me.

Her help isn't needed however as we see the crowd part and a lone paramedic make his way towards us.

"Right my dear let me have a wee look at this?" He

brings my arm down and I welcome the short-lived relief as he takes a quick look at my cut and puts my arm back up again.

"What's your name honey?"

"Gina."

"Right, Gina, I'm going to patch this up for the time being and get you transferred to A&E. There are a few shards of glass in there and you'll need a couple of stitches."

I look at Charlie who is as white as a sheet. "It's okay Charlie I'm fine. Would one of you contact Steven?"

"I already called him," says Sarah.

"Can I have my phone back please Sarah?" She seems to have forgotten she had it because it takes her a second to register.

"Oh, yes, sorry. Here you go." She seems a bit flustered, not her usual stoical self.

"Sarah is everything okay?"

"Yes, but I really want to get you out of here." She turns to the paramedic.

"Can I just take her to the hospital? It's less than a mile from here and I have a car with me."

"Absolutely. As soon as I've bandaged Gina up. I'm a first responder and only here on a bike so you'd have to wait for an ambulance anyway."

Sarah nods at him and pulls her own phone out of

her pocket as the paramedic tends to my hand, which is now starting to hurt like hell. The crowd around us has dissipated since the show is not as exciting as they first thought.

CHAPTER 19

I HATE HOSPITALS SO thankfully the A&E department at Glasgow's Royal Infirmary wasn't very busy. It was only a little after three in the afternoon on a Thursday anyway. Had it been Friday or Saturday night you could bet your last penny it would have been heaving.

As it happens, I was seen within half an hour. A nurse cleared the glass out of my hand and I now have three stitches on my palm. The area was numbed so right now I am enjoying some pain free time. I have to go back in a few days to have it checked.

Sarah brought Charlie and I back to Steven's apartment and Mark came to pick Charlie up. She left about half an hour ago and Sarah is now off doing her thing keeping an eye on me from afar. She was extremely tight lipped the whole time we were in the hospital and on the way back here. I think me having that fall shook her, but I'm sure she has seen worse, she was a bloody soldier. I texted Steven to let him know I was home and he replied that he will be a little late tonight. I have to say I am damn pissed at him. He must have got Sarah's message today about what happened to me.

I busy myself making some dinner the best I can with this stupid bandage on my hand and plant myself in front of the TV. I'm absentmindedly flicking through the channels when I hear the front door open.

"Steven?" I call out.

"Yeah babe I'm home sorry I was so late. I have something to tell you." I hear him at the hall cupboard putting his jacket and shoes away. My God even that seems more important. I'm starting to feel very sorry for myself.

"How was your day gorgeous?" He says as he walks into the TV room.

"Are you fucking kidding me right now?" I shout.

"Woah, back up what the hell have I done." He holds his hands up and so do I. The colour immediately drains from his face and he stalks straight to me. "Gina what happened?"

"Oh my God, Sarah called you and left a message for you, didn't you get it?"

"Sarah didn't call me at all today Gina. You know

fine well if I had gotten any sort of call like that I would have been right there. Now will you tell me what happened?"

I relay the story to him as he sits beside me on the couch holding my hand.

"Oh, Gina, I'm so sorry. I should have been there."

"Well obviously you didn't know. I'm okay it was just a stupid accident."

"But I should have known. This really isn't good enough Gina. How am I supposed to let you out of my sight when I can't guarantee your safety?"

I feel like a little kid, like I can't take care of myself, although looking at my hand I can see why he might think that.

"Steven you can't be with me every single second of the day. Sarah was there, she was with us the whole time, even when I didn't see her. I'm fine, it was an accident."

He closes his eyes. "I wish this would all just go away Gina. I have this constant fear in the back of my mind that something terrible is going to happen to you."

"Listen to me Steven, I understand why you feel like this, I know Colin is a bad guy but please believe me when I say I would never put myself at risk. Nick and his people are good at what they do so we have to leave this to them and trust them with it. You said we have to act normal. Well accidents are normal."

He looks at me and shakes his head, a slight smile forming on his lips. "You make things sound so easy Gina. You're a right wee optimist aren't you?"

I laugh. "What are we bloody like? I swear if things ever do start to run smoothly for us it just won't seem normal."

Steven pulls me in to him and kisses me. "And this brings me to what I need to tell you. I'm so sorry and the timing could not be worse. I've been asked to tender for the contract in Seattle."

I can't hide the disappointment in my eyes. "That's wonderful Steven. You said this was a big project."

"I'm not taking it," he says flatly.

"Why? Please don't mess up your opportunities because of this Steven. You'll be doing exactly what he wants. He wants to try and ruin you and you will be playing right into his hands."

"I know you are right, damn woman why do you need to be right?" His smile doesn't reach his eyes this time and I know he is fighting a losing battle with himself.

"How long will you be gone?"

"Only three days and I don't need to go until next week."

I can tell by the little spark in his eyes that he is actually excited about this. It's his job; it's what he's good at.

"Listen, if it makes you feel better, I can go and stay with my parents while you are away or even better still with Charlie and Mark. No one would know I was in Edinburgh."

"That sounds like a good idea and it would certainly make me feel better about leaving you."

"Sorted then. Get your trip organised. Now would you like some dinner?"

He flashes that wicked grin at me that says he wants something else entirely and I'm caught off guard when he grabs me round the waist and lifts me off the couch.

"I want you," he laughs as he makes a run for the stairs like the caveman he is.

CHAPTER 20

CHARLIE AND MARK LIVE on a street in Edinburgh not dissimilar to Steven's in Glasgow. The building overlooks a park and is a four-storey sandstone town house. They live in a flat on the ground floor, and as with most old buildings in the capital, it has that unmistakable black soot staining to the stone. The whole place has such character and I can see why Charlie loves living here. This is the first time I have visited this house. Charlie and Mark both sold their own places and pooled their finances when Charlie found out she was pregnant, so they have only lived here for a few months.

"Right Gina, call me as soon as you are ready to come back. Steven will be home on Friday night." Gerry smiles at me from the driver's seat of the Bentley.

"Thanks Gerry. This is going to be a refreshing few days."

"You're welcome and remember if you need anything all you need to do is call. I'm at your disposal."

"It's okay, I think I'm going to stay here until Steven's back."

I get out of the car and grab my bag from the back seat. "See you Gerry, thanks for the lift."

"Bye Gina, see you on Friday." I close the car door and head to Charlie's building. I feel relieved that I can leave the drama and constant looking-over-my shoulder behind for a few days. The only people who know I'm here are Charlie and Mark, Steven, Gerry and Nick. Sarah and Peter don't even know where I am and somehow that feels liberating.

A smiling Charlie greets me at the door.

"Oh, my darling I'm so glad you are here." She pulls me into a hug then drags me through the door. I can smell something delicious, like home baking. Charlotte Olsson does not bake.

"Charlie are you baking?"

"Yeah, I've made a coffee cake. I'm bored stiff Gina. I swear I have only been on maternity leave for three days and I want to go back to work already." She leads me in to the kitchen and the smell really hits me.

"Charlie this smells amazing. Get the coffee on."

"On it already honey." She smiles as she holds up the French press filled with coffee. She pours us both a cup and comes to join me at the table.

"Your flat is lovely Charlie."

"It really is isn't it? I fell in love with it as soon as I saw it on the estate agent's website. It took me a while to convince Mark though. We had to use every penny we had to make sure our mortgage payments were as low as possible. So, how's the hand? It doesn't seem like a week ago that happened."

I hold up my hand which now only has a small dressing over the cut. "I got the stitches out this morning after Steven left for the airport," I say with a heavy heart. Steven has only been gone for less than six hours and already I am pining. He won't even have landed in Seattle yet. Charlie looks like she is about to slap me.

"Come on honey, he's not fled the country. Well…technically he has but he's coming back. Now come on stop stressing me out woman, I need a distraction for the next few days and I'm not looking at that sour face."

"Sorry. I'm..."

"You're what?"

"I'm in love Charlie," I whisper and look away from her a little embarrassed.

She stands up and does a little happy dance

swinging her hands out in front of her. "Go Gina. Go Gina. Go Gina," she chants.

"Okay, okay calm down, I'm not delivering another baby." I try to be as light-hearted about that traumatic experience as I can, but it is still raw in my mind. I know in time the feeling of betrayal will fade and I will come to terms with it, hell maybe someday I can even laugh about it.

Charlie sits back down at the table, a little out of breath. "Sorry honey I'm just really happy for you. You deserve to be happy. Now do you want a tour?"

"Yes please. This place is awesome."

"I'll show you round then we can go out and get dinner. Mark is giving a presentation over at the zoo tonight so he won't be back until late."

***

As we sit in the Chinese restaurant at the end of Charlie's street, chatting back and forth, I get a really uneasy feeling that we are being watched. I know it's crazy, I think Steven's paranoia is rubbing off on me. No one knows I'm here, I'm safe.

"Gina, are you okay? You've been acting really strange since you got here today."

"I'm sorry Charlie, I just can't shake this feeling that someone is watching me. I know no one knows I'm here but it won't go away."

Charlie puts her hand on mine. "Honey I think you just miss your man and all this bodyguard stuff doesn't help. Speaking of your man, have you heard from Steven yet?"

"He had to get a domestic flight to London and then a connecting flight to Seattle. There are no direct flights from Glasgow. I think it's about a 17-hour journey. He called when he got to Heathrow, but he won't get to Seattle until the early hours of the morning. Well, our morning."

"Things will be fine honey. You'll probably feel better when you hear from him. We are going out for a girly night tomorrow night. Thursday's are as good in Edinburgh as they are in Glasgow. A few of the girls from my office are going to join us. I've booked us a table at The Witchery then we'll see where our feet take us after that. It won't be too far though or my feet will be like balloons."

"Sounds good to me."

We clink our glasses together and carry on eating. We talk about everything and anything and before long my feelings of paranoia slip to the back of my mind.

CHAPTER 21

BABY GEORGIE IS GOING to be one lucky little madam when she finally makes an appearance. Charlie and Mark have been busy decorating the nursery for the last month and it looks like something out of the pages of 'Beautiful Homes' magazine. The walls are painted white and, like the rest of the apartment, there is a beautiful solid oak floor. All the furniture is solid oak including the cot, which could sleep about eight babies. There are little pink accessories and toys all over and Georgie's name, in large pink gingham padded letters, is assembled on the wall above her cot. The place is simply stunning. I'm helping Charlie put away the last of the nappies and wipes and tiny little outfits.

"Where do you want these Charlie?" I ask holding up a box of baby wipes.

"Ooh, wait a minute I have something to put them in." She leaves the room for a moment and returns with a pink wipe dispenser.

"God Charlie it's like a pink palace for a little princess in here."

"I know and I bloody love it." Her face is positively glowing and her happiness is infectious. I feel myself smiling.

"So did you hear from lover boy last night then?" Charlie asks as she puts a little pink tutu dress on the tiniest clothes hanger I have ever seen.

"Yeah, he called just after midnight, but it was a very short conversation. I think he'd literally just got off the plane. He sounded exhausted. It was nice to hear his voice and he said he would call me this morning when he's had a chance to get settled."

"Well, you know what, I'm glad you're here honey even if you are just using me," she laughs and gets up from the floor.

"If you can't use your friends who can you use?"

"Let's get dressed and grab some breakfast. I need to go and pick up Georgie's pushchair today, so you can give me a hand with that, and then there is something I want to show you."

"Tell me what it is Charlie I can't take any more suspense; my nerves are shot to hell right now."

"Oh it wasn't going to be a massive surprise

anyway. I have a friend who is a keen amateur photographer and he is showing some of his work at a little gallery. It's like a showcase of Edinburgh's sights and his pictures are amazing. I really think you'll like it."

This is something I'm actually looking forward to. I would love to be at a stage in my career to be showing my photos in a gallery.

"Thanks Charlie, I'd love to see it."

"I knew you'd like it."

Our conversation is cut short by the shrill of my phone ringing in my pocket.

"It's Steven," I say to Charlie, running from the nursery and into the spare room with a flutter in my belly. I answer as soon as I have shut the door behind me.

"Hello."

"Hi gorgeous." The sound of his voice gives me goose bumps.

"Hi yourself. I miss you."

"Oh babe you have no idea. This hotel room is so empty. I want to touch you."

"Me too, I'm counting the hours. Can't wait till your home tomorrow"

"Well technically it's still Wednesday here, at least for another five minutes anyway."

"You won't be there long enough to adjust to the

time zone so for you it's almost eight in the morning on THURSDAY."

He gives a little laugh. "Got me on a technicality. So what have you and Charlie been up to?"

"We went out for dinner last night and this morning I've been helping her put all her baby stuff away. Steven you would not believe the size of some of these wee outfits, they are tiny." I don't tell him about my paranoia at dinner last night. It wouldn't serve any purpose for him to worry about me when he is four thousand miles and eight time zones away. I'm also enjoying the freedom of not having someone constantly monitoring me. "Oh…and she's arranged to take me to a gallery where a friend is showing his photos. I'd love to do that. Then we are off on a girly night out tonight."

"She really is keeping you busy. I better watch out or you'll forget I exist."

"Sorry who is this?" I laugh.

"Watch it MISSY," he says with a sigh behind the words. I can hear the longing in his voice and it makes me miss him even more.

I try to stay upbeat. "So what are your plans?"

"I'm off to survey the site first thing in the morning along with a rep from the building company I use in the States. I'll be meeting with the client's reps around lunchtime. Then it's off to the airport to come home to you. I have a six-hour stopover in London so I'm going to squeeze in a meeting before I head back to Glasgow."

"I'm knackered just listening to you. It's a lot to squash into a couple of days."

"Well hopefully it's all quick enough that I won't suffer too much with jet lag."

I really don't want to hang up the phone. I could gladly sit here the whole day talking about utterly mundane things with him just so that I can hear his voice. He lets out a long sigh.

"Are you okay?" I ask.

"Yeah. I really need to get on with some work and I'm damn near falling asleep on my feet tonight, but I don't want to go."

"I know; I don't want to go either."

"I'll be back soon enough. Go and get ready for your day out and have fun."

"I'm looking forward to it. Okay I'm off. Take care handsome call me whenever you feel the need to."

He pauses for a moment and as I'm starting to think the line has gone dead he speaks. "I love you my darling Gina."

"I love you too."

I sit staring at the phone for a long time. I'm absolutely head over heels in love with this man and it still shocks me sometimes.

I find Charlie in the kitchen and she's not alone. Mark is sitting at the kitchen table. He has his hands on either side of her bump and he is singing to the baby. It is the sweetest thing I have ever seen. These two melt my heart.

"Sorry guys."

"It's okay Gina, I'm heading off to work now. You girls enjoy your day." Mark kisses Charlie on the top of her head, grabs a travel mug from the counter and heads out the door.

"You two are so sweet," I say as Charlie sorts out her bag on the table.

"Oh stop it, you know I don't do sweet," she says with a smile then laughs. "We are kind of cute aren't we?"

We both hit a fit of the giggles. "You're nuts Charlie."

"Oh I don't need you to tell me that honey, now are you ready to go?"

"Lead the way darling."

***

The picture of Edinburgh Castle at night is absolutely stunning. The walls of the castle are lit up from below and the sky above it looks like it's on fire. It looks so dramatic. This is one of a collection of twelve photographs being shown by Charlie's friend

Jonathan. The others follow in the same vein. They are of all different landmarks around Edinburgh and I have to say he is a talented guy. He has managed to capture so much feeling and energy in his photographs. I can feel what it would have been like to look through the viewfinder of his camera as he took the shot. Another picture that catches my eye is of the Sir Walter Scott Monument. It's in black and white with a very dark and stormy feel to it. I shiver slightly as I look at it. It's like looking into the window of my mind in the months before I met Steven. I don't ever want to go back there. Now I feel more like the sky above the castle, on fire and ready to face the world.

"Charlie these are absolutely stunning."

"I told you he was good didn't I?"

"He's brilliant. He captures so much emotion in his pictures. How long has he been doing this?"

"About a year."

"Is that all? He's a natural."

Charlie pins me with that stare of hers. She's up to something, I can tell by the slight curve of her mouth and the way she narrows her eyes at me

"What?" I ask, slightly suspicious.

"Do you know why I really brought you here Gina?"

"Well I did think you were showing me your friend's work but now I'm not so sure."

"How long have you been doing photography?"

"As a career, about six years but really I haven't been without a camera since I was about twelve. Where are you going with this Charlie?"

"Why have you never done this? Your photos are amazing Gina. Those ones you took on Harris are bloody stunning, especially the ones of the northern lights."

"Oh Charlie no one wants to see my pictures."

She does not look amused. "Will you please stop putting yourself down and just learn to take a compliment once in a while. You are very good at what you do, and I really think you could go places. Something like this would be perfect for showcasing it."

"Do you really think so? I've never even entertained the idea of showing off my work in a gallery."

"Well now you can see that it is possible. Come with me. Jonathan put in a good word with the gallery owner and she wants to meet you."

The prospect fills me with fear. "Charlie no I have nothing prepared."

My protestations fall on deaf ears and she strides across the dark wooden floor of the gallery dragging me behind. As we reach the tiny office at the back, I see a tall woman with ash blonde hair pulled tightly into a bun. She is very slim and elegant.

"Hi there ladies how can I help you?"

"Hi, my name is Charlie. Jonathan said he had spoken to you about my friend Gina."

"Ah yes that he did. So, you must be Gina? It's a pleasure to meet you. My name is Ellen. Would you like to come into my office and we can have a wee chat? I've heard good things about you Gina."

I'm rather taken aback by this. When I decided to spend a few stress-free days with my best friend I should have known better. Charlie Olsson doesn't do things by half that's for sure.

CHAPTER 22

"ARE YOU ABOUT READY Gina? The taxi will be here in five minutes," Charlie's voice echoes from the kitchen.

"Two minutes honey," I call back. I put the finishing touches to my makeup and check myself in the full-length mirror on the back of the door.

"Yeah you'll do," I say to my reflection, smiling.

I can't believe the events of today. I left the gallery on Princes Street with a pending contract to show some of my pictures at an exhibition in Kelvingrove Art Gallery in Glasgow celebrating local artists and photographers. I was stunned when Ellen told me. She said she had looked at my website and, even though it is mostly portraits that are on there, she said she could see I was good at what I do. She said it is not just about capturing the image but the emotion behind it as well.

It doesn't matter if it is a human being, animal or inanimate object, if you don't show the emotion the picture is worthless. When I told her about the trip to Harris and the pictures I took of the Aurora and the beach she was extremely interested and asked me to send her copies of my work so that she can put them forward for consideration to be included in the exhibition. I walked out of that place with the biggest smile on my face.

I can't wait to tell Steven. I stop before leaving the bedroom and send off a quick text to him. I don't know if he will get it right now but even if it's tomorrow when he lands in London it doesn't matter.

Hey babe can't wait to see you. I have some great news to tell you. G x

I put my phone and a lipstick in my bag and head out to find Charlie. She's in the kitchen on her phone with Mark, I assume, since she keeps saying things like 'yes babe I'll be careful' and 'no I don't have heels on', even though she does have heels on. She looks at me and taps her foot on the floor winking at me and hangs up just as the taxi driver sounds his horn outside.

"All right babe lets go."

"What you going to do about the shoes? Mark will be here when we get home."

She holds up her bag, which could fit a small dog,

and laughs. "In this here bag I have a pair of flat ballet pumps. My heels will go in here when my feet can no longer handle the strain."

"You're a funny girl Charlie, now let's go I'm starving."

***

The taxi ride to The Witchery is only a five-minute journey from Charlie's house. The building is over four centuries old and is really rather spooky at night. Charlie gives her name for the reservation and we are seated at a long table with a full-length booth seat along one side and four chairs along the other. No one else is here yet so we order some drinks.

"What you having babe, your usual G and T?" Charlie asks as she orders herself a fresh orange.

"Nope I'm staying sober with you tonight honey, so I'll have the same please," I say to the waitress.

"Aww thanks darling that's so nice of you. It's good I'll at least have someone to talk to who can actually hold a conversation. You'll see what I mean when this bunch of pissheads turn up." I have to laugh at her analysis of her workmates.

"I swear Gina this lot could drink a guy under the table. They are worse than us when we were at Uni and that is saying something."

"Oh well this night should be interesting then."

And no sooner have I said that than four rather loud young ladies join us at the table, the rest of the restaurant patrons turning to see who is making such a racket. Interesting may be too soft a word for what this night may become.

***

The night is in full swing now. I have gotten to know Charlie's workmates and, although they are loud and could drink a rugby team under the table, they are a nice bunch of girls and they love Charlie to bits. They are all a lot younger than us aged between twenty-one and twenty-three and it shows. They are so full of energy and I hate to admit that a tiny part of me is a little jealous. Dinner was absolutely amazing and we are now in a pub on the Royal Mile.

"Right who's having shots?" Shouts Shelly, a very fiery redhead.

"Me," the other three shout in chorus.

"Gina what about you?"

"No I'll have what Charlie's having."

"Suit yourself, lightweight." Shelly laughs as she totters to the bar on heels that make her about five inches taller than she actually is. I can feel my feet hurt watching her negotiate the tiled floor. The other three girls get stuck into a conversation about their nails.

"Charlie this wee pub is fab. I'm starting to have a

new appreciation for Edinburgh."

"Mark and I come here quite a lot. It's always busy and that's a good sign. The busier the pub the better the atmosphere, as you well know."

I remember the fantastic pub we both worked in when we were in third year at Uni and it was always busy. It was close to where Charlie lived on Byers Road in Glasgow and most weekends I used to stay at her place because it was easier than getting a taxi home.

"Oh I remember. What's going on over there?" I nod in the direction of a little nook in the corner where some equipment is being moved and tested.

"There's live music in here every night. They have all different people playing everything and anything."

I have a feeling I'm going to enjoy this night out. I pull my phone from my bag to check the time and notice I have a text from Steven. My stomach flips.

Hope you are having a good time beautiful. Can't wait to see you tomorrow. xx

I smile so wide I think my face might split.

"Hey that's the biggest smile I've seen on your face in a long time Gina. Was that Steven?"

"Yeah. He can't wait to see me tomorrow. I miss him Charlie. Do you think it's too soon to be feeling like that?"

"No way honey. When you know you just know. I can tell he makes you happy and he really is a nice guy."

"What time does the music start?"

I ask Charlie as Shelly totters back from the bar with a tray absolutely jam packed with little shot glasses in a whole array of vivid colours.

"It starts at ten. Jesus Christ Shelly did you get enough shots?"

"Och these are just for starters," she laughs and starts handing the shot glasses to her friends. They down four each, all one after another. God the stuff looks evil.

I lean over to Charlie. "I'm just going to the loo Charlie I won't be long."

"Okay honey. We'll still be here." She rolls her eyes and it makes me laugh. I grab my bag from the floor and make my way towards the toilet. As I walk, I look around the bar and smile as I wonder whether I could still pull a good pint. It is a quaint little place with dark wood everywhere and the old fashioned dark green upholstery that is symbolic of old-style pubs. As I look at the other side of the bar, I'm forced to do a double take. I could have sworn someone was watching me. I fear being on my own in a place I don't know is bringing back the paranoia again.

The toilets are virtually empty. The only people in

here are a couple of extremely drunk young girls trying, and failing, to put lipstick on. They are giggling like idiots at themselves. As I tend to my full bladder, I hear them leave and the place stays unusually quiet. It seems rather strange in a pub as busy as this that there isn't at least someone else in here at any one time.

When I'm finished, I grab my bag from the hook on the door and as I'm about to open the lock, I hear the taps run. Funny, I didn't hear anyone come in. I step out of the cubicle and see a woman washing her hands. She is dressed in rather manly looking clothes and has a baseball cap on. Her head is bent concentrating on washing her hands. I quickly wash mine and walk over to the dryer. It is one of these new hand dryers that could take a layer of your skin off. The thing is so loud I can't hear myself think.

A sharp pain rips through my upper thigh making me stagger to the side. I'm stunned to be looking in to familiar eyes when I can stand properly again.

"Sarah? What are you doing here? What's going on?" My head is spinning and everything is becoming blurry. I feel like I'm falling into darkness and I'm sure I hear her say *'I'm so sorry Gina'* as my body gives in to the blackness.

CHAPTER 23

OH GOD MY BRAIN feels like it is going to explode. I don't want to open my eyes. Why am I so sore? Why am I so cold? I can hear voices. Echoes from the other end of a tunnel. I try to listen, but I can't make out what they are saying. I open my eyes and let them adjust to the semi-darkness. I notice an awful smell. It's like I have been sleeping in a toilet. In fact, that's exactly what this place looks like. When I try to move my hand up to my head, I realise they are bound in front of me and whatever is binding them is cutting into my skin. I'm lying on what feels like an old sleeping bag. I can hear footsteps and when I look up, I find myself staring at Sarah. My last memory flashes before me and I realise this is not a dream. No this is real and I'm scared. I sit up and press my back to the wall.

"Sarah what's going on? Where are we?" My voice

sounds hoarse.

"Shut up Gina. If you know what's good for you, you'll shut up." She shakes her head and looks at the floor. "Please?" She whispers.

I'm so scared. This woman was supposed to protect me. What the hell has happened to make her do this? And how the hell did she know where I was?

As my mind tries to make sense of it all the answer to my question walks through the door. My breath catches in my throat and panic sets in. I can feel my body trembling from pure terror. Standing in front of me with a manic look in his eyes is Steven's dad, Colin.

"Oh you're awake. Fantastic. Sarah fuck off, I need a word with this wee bitch."

Sarah scurries away.

"Why are you doing this?" I ask and am met with a slap across the face.

"Shut the fuck up. You'll speak when I tell you."

I bring my hands up and rub my cheek. I can feel the pain spreading across my face like fire and my binds bite deeper into my skin the more I move. Knowing what this man is capable of terrifies me.

"So, finally I get to meet the wee gold-digger. You fair landed on your feet didn't you? Meeting the millionaire. Yeah, the wee fucker who ruined my life."

His voice is like venom. I'm so angry. How dare he

say that?

"He did nothing to deserve any of this you bastard," I shout. Where that came from I don't know but what I do know is that I'm about to regret it.

Anger flares in his eyes and he rushes at me grabbing me by the throat and pushing me further into the wall. "You know nothing. Fucking nothing. He lost me everything." He pushes me hard as he lets go of me, banging my head on the wall, and storms out. I hear a door banging and then there is silence.

My mind is racing and I have so many images flashing around in there that it is making me feel dizzy. I think about Steven and Charlie. I wonder how long I have been gone. Charlie will be frantic. Steven probably doesn't even know I'm missing. I don't even know if I'm still in Edinburgh. God I could be anywhere. As I'm wondering where Colin has gone, Sarah comes back. She doesn't look at me but instead busies herself in the opposite corner.

"Sarah, where are we?"

She doesn't answer.

"Sarah, will you please talk to me? What is going on? How did you end up in all this?" I see her shoulders slump. She turns to me and looks at me. There is daylight creeping in through the cracks in the boarded-up windows and I can see she has tears in her eyes.

"Please Gina, I can't speak to you."

"Sarah what does he have over you? How do you even know him?"

"For fuck sake Gina, will you shut up? Look I'm sorry this had to happen like this but if he finds me talking to you..." She trails off and I see torment in her eyes.

"What has he done to you?" I ask in a low voice. She simply shakes her head and walks out. I might actually die here and no one will even know. I can't believe this is happening. I thought what happened with Abby was the scariest thing I would ever experience but this is a million times worse. This man is a murderer.

Colin storms back in carrying a roll of black duct tape and some plastic cable ties. I sink as far back as I can, but he comes over to me and grabs my tied hands. I try to struggle free but he's so strong.

"Fucking stay still or I'll knock you out." His breath is disgusting and his teeth are awful, but I look up at him and into a pair of strikingly deep blue eyes. I stop struggling and gasp. Oh my God it is like looking into Steven's eyes. I can't move.

Colin binds my ankles together with the cable ties then puts another through the gap and attaches them to the ones on my wrists so that I can't move. He tears a piece of tape off and forces it over my mouth. He stands up and pulls a folding chair from somewhere in the shadows and sits in front of me.

"Ah silence is golden. Now I can get a word in. Fucking women don't know when to shut up." He sits back and links his fingers behind his head, crossing one foot over the opposite knee.

"You're a good looking wee lassie I'll give him that. So you think you know all about me eh? No hen, you don't. Lover boy won't have told you everything, he's too embarrassed you see." He shifts his position so that he has both feet on the floor and his elbows on his knees. "I'm gonna make sure you never want to see him again. And when I'm done with you, he'll never want to look at you again."

This man is pure evil. I was right. His endgame is to ruin any chance Steven has to be happy. Colin laughs.

"Yeah I made some good money out of that wee bastard, it was the least he could do after ruining my life."

I can feel tears prick my eyes. I close them against the stinging.

"Yeah you'll fucking listen alright hen." His words come out of his mouth on a sneer. I am utterly repulsed by him.

"There's always some way to make a living out of kids. There's some right fucked up people out there. Not me you see, I'm not a peado. Nah weans don't float my boat but it's not hard to find the ones that are. Stick an ad in the right place and they'll come running."

I feel like I'm going to be sick. The tears are free flowing down my cheeks. I watch as he takes a pack of cigarettes out of his pocket and proceeds to light one. He takes a long draw on it and leans forward, blowing the smoke right in my face. It burns my nostrils and stings my eyes.

"At first it was the ones that wanted to touch him, I never let it go any further than that mind, I'm not that bad. But over time we cornered a wee niche in the market. He made a good naked slave. Now that was where the money was. Aye it was good for a while, till he got me the jail that is. Ah we could have been business partners and made a fortune, but he ruined that didn't he."

I'm sobbing so hard and my mouth hurts from the tape. I try to scream but the sound is muffled. I throw myself down onto the sleeping bags and close my eyes. I wish Steven had been strong enough to tell me himself. I fear I may not make it out of this alive to be able to help him through this. Colin is on his feet now and laughing at me. He kneels down right next to me and puts his face right in mine. I keep my eyes closed tight. I don't want to see him.

"You don't want a dirty wee boy in your bed do

you Gina? Oh if you'd seen some of the things he did to make his dad proud. Now sweet dreams hen, you're gonna need all the energy you've got."

The smell of the cigarette on his breath makes me want to heave. He stubs it out on the wall above me. I feel the same sharp stabbing pain in my leg again and I start to drift towards the darkness all the while calling Steven's name until there is nothing.

CHAPTER 24

"BABY MINE DON'T YOU cry. Baby mine dry your eyes. Rest your head close to my heart. Never to part. Baby of mine."

The voice I can hear through the fog is beautiful but full of lamentation. I open my eyes. My head is pounding and I feel sick. It is unbearably cold. My bladder feels like it is going to burst and my trousers feel damp. Oh God have I been so out of it I have peed myself? Trying to open my mouth I realise it is still taped shut. I haul myself up and the singing stops. I try to focus on the little light on the opposite side of the room. It illuminates the figure sitting beside it. Sarah is watching me. We sit staring at each other for a long moment. She stands up and comes to me. As she crouches down beside me I back away from her. I'm scared and I can't trust her.

"I'm going to take the tape off Gina. You need to drink, you've been here for almost three days."

This revelation shocks me. And it explains the damp trousers. I feel totally degraded. How could Sarah let this happen? I must have been under the influence of whatever drugs they gave me for hours and hours at a time. She starts to peel off the tape, but it hurts too much and I pull my face away from her.

"I'll get some water." She disappears for a moment and returns with a bottle of water and a dirty rag.

I watch as she wets the cloth and then starts to dab at the sides of the tape against my skin. I can feel it start to ease away from my face and as my lips are freed, I take in huge gulps of air. I can't help but start to cry in great heaving sobs.

"Sshh Gina please? If he knows I've done this he'll do... please just don't make too much noise." She looks worried, scared even. I can tell there is something horrible going on and I know I need to try to reach out to her and find out what it is, it may be my only way out of here alive.

"Here take a drink Gina."

I drink from the offered bottle, grateful for the chilled water sliding over my parched palate. My stomach growls and cramps with hunger pains. Sarah takes the bottle away.

"Sarah please tell me why you are doing this? I

don't think you really want to be here do you?"

"Please Gina don't ask me that, I can't tell you." She has such a haunted expression on her face.

"I can make sure everything is okay for you if I get out of this. I promise I'll tell them you helped me. I don't think you'd be here unless he had something over you."

She looks down at the bottle in her hand, twisting it round and round. "Gina I'm so sorry. I didn't want this to happen. I wouldn't be here if..." She stops talking, gets up and makes her way to the door, disappearing for a few seconds. When she comes back, she sits beside me with her back against the wall.

"He has my daughter Gina." Her voice is almost a whisper and she starts to cry.

"Oh Sarah I'm so sorry. How did you end up involved in all this?" I truly am sorry for her. My first instinct was right. I knew she would never have done this willingly.

"He took her the day before you hurt your hand. He came to my home that night. I found him in Megan's bedroom. He told me I had to get your phone and put a tracker on it. When you fell and cut your hand, I managed to get your phone after you dropped it. I thought that was all, but he kept changing the rules. He said if I didn't do as he said he would cut her throat. She's my baby Gina I can't let anything happen to her." Sarah completely breaks down in tears beside me. I can't even put my hands up to comfort her.

"Hey I understand. I assume you don't know where he has her?"

She shakes her head. "He said I will get her back when he is finished with you and Steven. I can't let anything happen to him before I find out where she is. He is the only one who knows. When I get her back the bastard can rot in hell. She's only three years old Gina, she'll be terrified."

"Where are we Sarah?"

"Kelvingrove Park. The disused toilet blocks at the far end of the park."

"What? You mean to say I have been so close to Steven this whole time. Sarah, he will be frantic. And what about poor Charlie? She doesn't need the stress of this right now. And my parents, this will end them." Right now, in this moment of clarity, I realise how many people I have in my life who love me. I'm determined I'm going to survive this.

"He is frantic Gina. No one knows I'm involved in this. I have been at Steven's apartment when I haven't been here." She looks truly remorseful. "Believe me it is killing me seeing how much your disappearance is affecting everyone. Knowing that I could end it is the worst thing. I want to tell them where you are every time I'm there but I can't. Colin wants me to keep an eye on the operation and feed him information. I'm giving him some but it's not the right information. I don't know what to do Gina. I can only hold him off so long."

I think about Steven worrying about me and blaming himself for this happening, about my parents, if they have even been told. It wouldn't surprise me if Steven tried to spare their feelings by not telling them. It would be easy enough for Sarah to let on where I am and have the police storm the place, but then she would never find her daughter.

"I'll do everything I can to help you Sarah. I think you need to tell Steven and Nick what has happened. Nick is good he'll be able to help you."

"Oh come on Gina. They'll just send the police charging in here to arrest him and he'll never talk."

"No they won't, not if they know a child's life is in danger. You have to find a way to let Steven know I'm okay." I have an idea, but I really need to pee so that I can concentrate. "Can you untie my hands Sarah I really need to pee? Just cut the one holding these two together so that I can at least stand up. I promise I won't do anything."

Sarah pulls a little folding knife from her pocket and cuts the tie that holds my hands to my ankles. She also removes the ones on my wrists and I can see garish red welts in both of them. I immediately stretch out my legs and my arms and arch my back. It's such a relief.

"Where can I go?"

"There's a bucket over here." She helps me up and I hop over to the other side of the room. I relieve myself and the feeling is so good. The smell from my clothes however is disgusting and I feel disgusting.

"When is he due back?"

She looks at her watch. "He said he'd be back by midday. It's ten thirty right now."

"Right we have some time. You have to call Steven so that I can speak to him. I will explain everything to him, you have to trust me Sarah. When Steven finds out what he did to you he will understand. He won't blame you, he knows what that monster is capable of." I can see that she is unsure about this. I know her only priority is her daughter right now. "Please Sarah I promise I won't let anything happen to you or Megan, but I need to let them know I'm okay."

"I'll call but please don't let Megan down Gina, she's all I have left."

"I promise." I try to sound as reassuring as I can, but I have no Idea what is going to happen when I speak to Steven. She walks over to where the little light sits on the floor and pulls out a phone from a duffel bag next to it. She comes back and hands it to me and I see that it is mine. I look at her puzzled.

"All the trackers have been wiped. Your iCloud has

been disabled as well so none of the location apps work."

"Won't they be able to find out where the call is coming from anyway?"

"Yes, but it takes a few minutes to do that. Hopefully by that time you'll have explained enough to tell them not to come here."

I turn on the phone and wait for it to boot up. As soon as it does it starts going crazy with voicemail messages and texts, mostly from Steven and Charlie. I picture them desperately trying to find me and it hurts my heart. My parents will be devastated.

I find Steven's name in my contacts and tap the screen. I hold it to my ear as best I can with bound hands and my heart rate rises as I wait for the call to connect. As soon as it does tears spring to my eyes.

"Gina?" Steven's voice is hoarse.

"Steven," I whisper.

"Oh God Gina, where are you? Nick get fucking in here." I hear him shout.

"Steven stop," I shout. "I need you to stay as calm as possible and listen very carefully." I hear a commotion on the other end of the phone.

"Are you okay Gina?"

"I'm fine. Sarah is with me."

"What the fuck Gina, how? Where are you?" He asks again.

"Steven stop shouting I need to explain what has happened, but you have got to calm down and listen. Colin has me."

I hear a sharp intake of breath.

"He has taken Sarah's daughter. She doesn't know where he has her and if anything happens to him, she will never find out where she is. You have to try and find her before you come for me. I'm fine and as long as he doesn't know I have been in touch with you I will be okay."

He is silent for a long time, then I hear him let out a breath. "I need to tell Nick, he can help Gina. I think I know of some places where he might be holding the girl."

"Do what you need to do but please don't let anything happen to Megan. Sarah will fill you in when she gets there later okay."

I feel Sarah tense beside me and we both stop and listen. The sound of a car door closing makes us both jump and I immediately hang up the call and almost throw the phone at Sarah. She turns it off and manages to get it back in the bag as the outside door bangs and those footsteps that fill me with dread approach.

CHAPTER 25

"OH SHE'S STILL ALIVE then. Thought I'd fucking killed you. Now wouldn't that have been an interesting turn of events Sarah?" Colin looks from me to Sarah and back again. His expression darkens when he sees the tape gone from my mouth and my wrists free from my ankles.

"What the fuck did you do that for Sarah? Who said you could untie her?"

"She needed to use the toilet. I didn't untie her fully. She can't run away."

He lifts his huge dirty hand and whacks her across the face so hard she is knocked off her feet.

"If its money you want Steven can pay, you know he can," I say trying to divert his attention in case he does something terrible to Sarah. She is my lifeline, I'll never get out of here without her and her little girl needs her.

"Ppfftt come on you stupid girl. You know as well as I do if I wanted all his money, I could just take it. This isn't about money it's about revenge and I'm going to make sure he pays for what he did to me." Colin's eyes are like fire and he volleys a swift kick into my thigh. I cry out in pain. My blood is boiling, and it takes every ounce of strength I have left to keep my mouth shut.

"Right Sarah it's time you got back to your job. I want you to take something with you this time. Leave it at the front door or something just remember, you let on what's happening here and you know what'll happen."

Colin walks over to me and pulls a large hunting knife from his boot. He grabs a handful of my hair and chops it clean off. It happens so quickly that I'm shocked to see him standing there with my beautiful brown hair in his hand. He lifts the bag he came in with and pulls out a large manila envelope, opens it and drops the hair inside. He hands it to Sarah and ushers her out the door, all the while she is clutching her cheek where he slapped her. Then he returns to me, kneeling right down in front of me.

"That's a fucking warning. If he doesn't do what daddy tells him he'll be getting more than hair in the mail." He grabs my hands and strokes my fingers. I try to pull them away, but he squeezes my hands so tight I fear he will break them.

"Oh, you want a fight do you?" He says as he lets go of my hand and punches me on the side of the face. My vision is blurred as my head is jolted to the side and I feel my lip swell immediately. The searing hot pain travelling up my face is intense and as much as I don't want to show my weakness, I can't help the tears that run from my eyes.

"There you look better already. God that felt good," he says flexing his fingers in front of him. He grabs his roll of duct tape and puts a piece over my mouth again, then he replaces the cable ties that Sarah cut. "That should keep you quiet. I'll be back shortly don't be trying anything stupid now or I'll send him your fucking heart," he laughs a horrible, sinister laugh that chills me to the bone.

How could Steven ever think he would end up like this piece of shit? Colin walks out the door whistling, as casual as if he was leaving work for the day. As soon as he is gone, I let my emotions take over and cry until I'm so exhausted I drift off to sleep with the image of a frightened little boy being consumed by big black shadows.

***

I wake suddenly, feeling as though I'm flying through

the air.

"Get on your fucking feet bitch." Colin's words come at me through gritted teeth.

I'm hauled to my feet but because my hands are still bound to my ankles I can't stand up. He leans down and cuts the tie and I stand up straight, feeling my bones creak.

Before I can do anything, he hoists me over his shoulder and carries me out of the door and into the fresh air of the park. I take in deep breaths of the cold air, my nostrils and lungs burning as I try to fill them with as much of it as I can. He stops at the door. It's very dark outside from what I can make out in my upside-down state but there are plenty of streetlights. I feel him bend slightly and a car door opens. I'm thrown into the back seat and the door slams.

I'm lying here terrified. I don't know what is going on and as I try to sit up, he speeds away from the building, jolting me back down again. This is where he gets his revenge on Steven. I close my eyes and send up a silent prayer. I'm not even religious, I just want to go home.

The shrill of a mobile phone makes me jump and Colin answers.

"You're too late you wee fucker. She's not there anymore. You should have done what I asked. Her death will be on you and you can tell Sarah she better sleep with her eyes open from now on cos I'm coming to get her and her little princess."

He keeps up with the expletives and nasty threats as he snakes his way round the roads through the park. From my position on the backseat I can see he has the phone at his ear and is steering with one hand. I grab my opportunity. I launch myself at him pulling his dirty shirt with both hands as the cable tie digs in to my wrists. I pull with all the strength I have left and he loses control of the car. I'm hurtled off the back seat hitting the front seats then the floor as the car impacts on something. I feel a floating sensation in my stomach and as the second impact happens and I'm thrown around the car like a ragdoll. I realise I'm now lying on the ceiling. *Oh God the car is upside down.* I don't have any time to get my bearings before water starts to fill the inside of the car incredibly quickly. It is freezing cold and I'm finding it hard to focus. My mouth is still taped and my wrists and ankles are still bound. I try as hard as I can to kick the windows, but the car starts to sink further into the icy water. I reach up and rip the tape from my mouth and take the biggest breath of air my lungs will allow as the car goes under completely and I'm fully submerged. I keep trying to kick the windows out, but they won't budge. I haven't eaten for three days and I have no energy. My lungs are on fire and the water is stinging my wrists where the cable ties are scraping my skin. In my mind I'm screaming for Steven to save me, *'Please Steven help me. Help me. Help me'*. I can't hold this breath any longer. I have to let go. The silence is eerie and I close my eyes and say goodbye. I am at peace.

CHAPTER 26

EVERY TIME I COME up for air Colin bats me back down. His horrible grin getting wider with each push. His form is getting bigger as well. He is now the height of five men and this time when I come up his giant hand squashes me into the riverbed. The last thing I hear is his evil laugh. The last things I see are Steven's eyes.

I wake up from my nightmare, but I can't see. Everything is white. I can feel fingers touching my hand and I can hear... sobbing. Please don't cry.

"Gina, I love you. I'm so sorry. Can you ever forgive me?"

I feel a tear fall from my eye and I try to hold his hand.

"Gina can you hear me?"

'Yes. Yes, I can.' Why won't the words come out

of my mouth?

"Gina squeeze my hand."

'I am.'

"I can feel you, do it again."

"Steven." That's my voice saying his name. I try again. "Steven."

I can hear a lot of voices now, one in particular sounds angry. "Mr Parker you will need to step outside please we need to check her over."

"Gina can you hear me?"

"Yes. I want Steven. I need a drink."

"He can come back in when we are done."

As the muted light filters into my eyes I can see a nurse's face. Steven is still in the room pacing in defiance of her.

"Mr Parker, if you are going to insist on staying you are going to have to let us do our job. Gina needs to be checked over." Her voice is stern.

"Okay I'm sorry. I'll wait outside."

The nurse checks my eyes, chest, reflexes and grip and I am placed into a semi-seated position. I'm utterly exhausted, but I can see Steven outside the door and I can finally smile. I'm given a drink of water through a straw.

"Gina do you know where you are?" Asks the nurse by my side.

"Hospital."

"Do you know why you are here?"

"Yes. An accident."

The nurse beckons Steven back in. "Do you know who this man is?"

"My Steven."

Steven's face lights up and he comes to me. He sits down on the chair beside the bed and holds my hand. He looks like he has been through the wars.

"I thought I had lost you. Everyone was so worried."

"I'm so sorry Steven. So sorry."

He lifts my hand to his lips. "Don't you dare apologise."

"Right Gina I will be back in five minutes and I'm afraid I really am going to need some proper time alone with you then, okay?" She is talking to me but looking at Steven with narrowed eyes.

"Okay you win," Steven says and scowls back at her. As the door closes behind her Steven sticks his fingers up at it.

"That's not nice Steven," I say with a weak smile.

"Fucking Nurse Ratched there has had it in for me since she came on shift this morning."

I'm so happy to see him, to know that I'm still in the land of the living.

"Steven please tell me what happened? How long have I been here?"

"Gina you don't need to worry about anything. The people who need to be safe are."

I take a moment to process his words and remember Sarah. "Is Sarah's little girl okay?"

"Gina please, I'll tell you everything but don't put yourself under too much stress right now okay."

My whole body is sore and my limbs feel so heavy. I'm too exhausted to argue with him but not knowing what has happened is stressing me out. I feel my eyelids droop. I force them open again as I catch Steven's pained expression and am reminded of what Colin said, about what he did to that poor wee boy. Tears spring to my eyes as I imagine those beautiful blue eyes on a small, undernourished version of him and now I'm sobbing.

"Hey, hey it's okay. You are fine, you are here, a little battered and bruised maybe but you are fine."

"Oh Steven I know about..." I don't get to finish what I want to say as the nurse comes back in.

"Right Mr Parker, I need to deal with some delicate procedures now, would you give us half an hour please."

Steven nods and leans over to kiss my head. "I'm going to call Charlie and Mark and let them know you're awake. Your mum and dad are still here. I'll be here when you're done."

I really don't want him to leave. As soon as he is

out the door I pounce. "How long have I been here?"

"Oh honey you've been unconscious for a couple of days. You were very lucky you know."

Her voice is soft and calming. I smile slightly thinking about what might have been going on around me while I was out of it. I bet he has really been pissing off the staff, trying to get his own way.

"What happened to me?"

"Has Mr Parker not filled you in?" Her scowl is back as she mentions Steven. God she really doesn't like him.

"No, he hasn't. He thinks I'm a little china doll, that I need protecting. I really want to know."

"Let me get this catheter out and I'll tell you as much as I know." She goes about the business of draining fluid from the tube and removes the catheter in one swift movement. The feeling of total relief is amazing.

"Oh thank you, that feels so good. I thought I was going to pee myself."

"It feels like that because it sits in your bladder, so it always feels full."

She smiles at me. I give her a moment to discard the thing then jump right in again.

"So, tell me what happened?"

"Well from what I know of your case you almost drowned in the river Kelvin, inside an upturned car.

Well technically you did drown but there was apparently some good Samaritans who happened to witness the whole thing and luckily for you they knew CPR. They got you out of the car and saved your life. And all you have is some deep bruising, so you really are extremely lucky. No broken bones or anything. Someone must have been watching over you."

Oh God! I was dead! "How do you know all this? Did Steven tell you?"

"Honey it was in all the local papers on Monday. In fact, I'm pretty sure there was something on the news about it this morning. I think they are still trying to trace some family of the guy that died. Did you know who he was? They said you had been kidnapped."

My whole body shakes. Colin is dead? Oh my God I killed someone. I need to speak to Steven.

"I want Steven, I need to see him." My voice is shaking.

"You need to calm down Gina. Mr Parker will have to wait until we are finished here."

"Please call him Steven and stop being horrible to him."

She looks a little shocked at my outburst. I immediately feel bad. Steven has probably been an absolute nightmare to these poor people.

"I'm sorry. What's your name?"

"Sharon," she replies with a smile.

"Sharon I'm sorry. Has he been pissing you off?"

"He cares a great deal, that much is clear to see, but he keeps getting in the way and won't do as he is told." She gives a little laugh. "I'll get finished as quickly as I can here, you'll probably need to stay another night and all going well you'll be discharged at some point tomorrow."

"Thanks. I'm sure you'll be glad to be rid of us." The fact that she merely smiles at me as she goes about her business tells me that is most likely true. I must reprimand my overprotective boyfriend.

***

Steven is back by my side seconds after Sharon leaves. God he must have been pacing right outside the door. My mum and dad quickly follow him. As soon as mum sets her eyes on me, she is in tears. I'm very overwhelmed.

"Oh, my darling girl. I thought I'd lost you." Mum's voice is unbelievably quiet and I start to cry along with her.

"I'm fine mum, please don't cry." My head is thumping and I'm becoming increasingly tired, this crying is not helping matters.

"Honey we are just so glad you're okay. Carla she really needs to rest. Come on we can come back in the morning." That's my dad, ever the diplomat. He looks shattered.

"Yes okay, now listen," she says as she looks to Steven, "any problems and you have to call us straight away."

They all look like a good night's sleep is what they need. I have never seen my parents look so haggard in all my life.

"Go mum please I'm fine, it's all over now, he can't hurt us anymore." I look at Steven who is regarding me with wide eyes as he realises I know Colin is dead. I am exhausted, but I really want to know everything.

"Right we'll be back in the morning okay sweetheart." Says dad as he kisses me softly on my forehead. Mum follows suit and they both head for the door.

"I'll walk you down folks. I'll be back shortly Gina okay."

I nod at him as they all leave the room and as soon as the door closes, I feel my eyes droop. I fall into a strange sleep filled with the beautiful blue eyes of a neglected child and those of a cold-blooded killer.

CHAPTER 27

"STEVEN WILL YOU PLEASE sit down? Pacing around in circles is making me bloody dizzy."

He stops in the middle of the floor with his back to me. His hands at his sides make tight fists. He turns to me and I can see fury in his eyes.

"I am so fucking angry Gina. I should never have gone to Seattle while all this was going on. I should have known."

Having slept the whole night after mum and dad left, I have just finished recounting my ordeal and, to give him credit, he didn't utter a word. I dread what he is going to say or do now.

"How could you have known? As far as you were concerned I was fine. I was with my friend, no one was supposed to know I was there. Now you need to tell me what has gone on since the crash." I really want to know what has happened with Sarah and her little girl. Steven closes his eyes and sighs.

"Sarah and Megan are fine. He had the wee one holed up in his mum's old house. Apparently she died last month and the house is now up for sale. When you told me he had Megan it was one of the places we checked. I wish it had been the first but there were other places I thought she might be. The poor girl is traumatised. I don't think he did anything to her but being taken away from her mother is bad enough. He had left her there on her own while he was away checking on you. Sarah is fine, but she has terminated her employment with Nick."

"Oh poor Sarah. Please don't blame her Steven."

"I don't. I know that I would do the same if anything happened to a child of mine. Sarah's a good mother. Did you know her husband was killed in a car accident when Megan was a month old? He never got to meet her. The worst part about it was that he was just back from a tour of duty and was hit on a pedestrian crossing near his barracks because someone ran a red light."

My heart breaks. I could see the pain in her eyes when she talked about her daughter.

"That's so sad." I lift my hand to brush back a bit of stray hair and notice the bandages on my wrists for the first time. I stare at them for a moment.

"You did so much struggling the cable ties have ripped your skin to shreds," says Steven as he comes to sit beside me on the edge of the bed. He takes my hands and rubs my knuckles.

"I don't know what I would have done if anything had happened to you Gina." He leans in and kisses the top of my head.

"Steven, I know what he did to you," I whisper. I can't hold this in any longer. It tore my heart in two when Colin told me what he had put Steven through as a child.

"I thought he would tell you," he says, his voice low but heavy with sadness.

"Do you want to talk about it?"

He leans back slightly and then gets up and walks over to the window, staring out with his hands thrust in the pockets of his jeans. Rain is battering the window and the sky is as grey as the mood in this room.

"I told you he was evil Gina. I'm so sorry I didn't tell you, it's just... it makes me feel dirty. I spent so long living in fear of what horrible sleazy bastard he would have lined up for me next. I wanted to die on quite a few occasions during that time. I can't relive it all again, what's done is done and right now I'm fucking angry that I never got to knock the living shit out of him. I wanted to kill him myself." He bows his head and I can see his shoulders slump.

God this is awful. Steven is now in the same boat as me. He will never have the answers he needs. He will never have closure. I feel sick to my stomach.

"I didn't mean for this to happen Steven. He should be here to answer for this. I was just trying to get someone's attention, I really thought he was going to kill me."

"He was Gina."

His words make me gasp. "How do you know?" I ask, my voice on the edge of tears.

"He told me."

I can't breathe. I clamp my hand to my mouth; my entire body is shaking. Steven turns and looks at me.

"He said he was finished with the games and that I would find you where my mother was found. I swear Gina it is just as well he died because I'd probably be in jail for murder if he hadn't."

He comes over to me and sits beside me again. Lifting my hands in his, he presses a kiss to my knuckles. "I love you Gina and this last week has made me realise that you are stronger than anyone gives you credit for. More than I even gave you credit for. Sarah told me everything. How you kept calm and how she trusted you enough to open up about what had happened. You wouldn't be here had you not been the strong-willed person you are. I'm so proud of you."

"I was damn terrified Steven. Not for my own life

but because I might never see you again." I move over on my bed slightly, wincing a little as I lean on the thigh Colin kicked. I can only imagine the bruise that's there. I motion for him to lie next to me. He does and props his head up on his hand, touching my face with the other. I can't make him tell me what happened to him, but he needs to know I'm here if he ever wants to.

"Steven, I love you with all my heart, please believe that. I don't care what happened all those years ago, I want to live for now. I understand if you can't tell me but I'm here for you if you ever need to talk."

He smiles and wraps his arms around me as I lay my head on his shoulder. Closing my eyes, I listen to his heartbeat and the rain at the window and thank my lucky stars that I am here at all.

***

As I look at my best friend, I'm reminded just how grateful I am to have all these people around me who love me. Charlie looks tired and drained.

"Oh Charlie I'm so sorry. Please stop crying, I'm fine."

"I can't, even if I wanted to. My hormones are fucked up." She sniffs and I see an involuntary smile tug at her lips. When I smile back, she starts to laugh, so hard in fact, that she chokes on thin air.

"Bloody hell Gina," she splutters. "I hate you."

"Love you too honey."

She holds my hand and nods her head. "I'm so relieved you are okay Gina. I could never have lived with myself if anything had happened to you."

"How many times do I need to tell you this was not your fault Charlie? That man was a monster. I wanted to believe that there might have been some good in him, somewhere, but there wasn't. He was pure evil. I'm glad you weren't caught up in all this."

"Are you okay? I mean really okay?" Charlie taps her head. I roll my eyes.

"Yes Charlie my mental state is fine. It was traumatic but I have realised so much because of it. Believe me, I will never again take anything for granted in my life. Ever."

Charlie smiles and sits back in her chair. She looks about ready to pop and I can see she is exhausted. "I'm going to have to go soon honey. I have an antenatal appointment later today. I'm hoping the midwife is going to say, 'oh yes Charlie you are in labour let's get baby out'. I've still got four weeks left and I'm so fed up."

I feel for her, I really do.

"So, when are you getting released?"

"God Charlie you make it sound like I'm a prisoner."

She laughs. "Well you were for a wee while."

"Yeah don't remind me. The doctor said if all looks well on his next ward round that I will be able to leave today. I want this all to be over."

"I know honey. How is Steven doing?"

I lower my eyes as I think about him. He must have been terrified as a child to have those unspeakable things happen to him.

"He won't talk about it, but he is angry that he never got to tell his father what he really thought of him. I doubt it would have made much of a difference in the end, the man had such a black heart. He had no remorse. The bastard actually tried to justify what he did. The things Colin told me Charlie, it would turn your guts."

Charlie shakes her head as the door to my room opens and Mark comes in. "Hey Gina, how are you?" He says as he leans in and kisses my head.

"I'm fine Mark. I can't wait to get out of here though."

"Yeah, I'm not a fan of hospitals. I had a bad experience as a child when I was getting my tonsils out, so I try to avoid them if I can." Mark turns to Charlie. "Right babe, it's time for us to go if we want to make your appointment. We'll see you on Saturday Gina."

Saturday? My surprised expression registers with Mark as Charlie looks like she is going to murder her fiancé.

"Oh for goodness sake you two what the hell has he got planned? And don't either of you even try to bullshit me."

Charlie laughs and stands up. She kisses my forehead and drags Marks to the door. "Not telling you."

The door closes and I can hear her giggling outside.

"Bitch," I shout, laughing at her.

Then it is quiet again. Being alone is giving me too much room to think. I don't want to remember what happened to me and I want to think about what happened to Steven even less.

It is testament to his nature that he has turned into the amazingly strong person he is today. His life could so easily have gone the way so many others do who have been in the same situation as him. There is a common theory that abuse breeds abusers. I don't think that's true in most cases and certainly not in Steven's. He has questioned whether or not he will turn out like his father and he probably will for a long time to come but there is one huge difference between Colin and Steven. Steven knows what happened to him was wrong. Colin tried to justify it as a means to an end. He didn't acknowledge it as abuse, sexual or otherwise. No, I know Steven will never be like him and I will do everything I can to help him realise that.

And right on cue, as he consumes my mind, the man himself appears in my door, holding a huge bunch of fiery coloured gerbera daisies and wearing a massive smile that would melt the coldest of hearts.

CHAPTER 28

THE THING ABOUT BEING kidnapped and almost dying is that people look at you differently. I have caught Steven, too many times over the last few days, looking at me with uncertainty in his eyes. It's as though sometimes he can't believe I'm actually here.

At least now he is willing to touch me. The first day I was home from the hospital was unbearable and at one point I even wished I were back there. He wouldn't let me do anything, but he also wouldn't touch me. It was weird. When I was in my hospital bed, he had no problem holding my hand or lying down beside me but as soon as I was home, I became the china doll again. I slept by myself on that first night and found Steven asleep in the tub chair when I woke up. He looked very uncomfortable and nearly had a heart attack when I went and crawled into his lap.

We have both agreed that we will go and see Nate together today. I normally go to my appointments by myself but this time it's different. This session is not going to be the same as all the rest. This one is going to be our turning point. My bruises are healing, slowly, with the exception of my thigh that is still sporting a huge purple bruise. I was told at the hospital that there was very deep tissue bruising and that it would get worse before it gets better. I'm also glad that the nightmares are starting to dissipate a little. I can get a full night of unbroken sleep without one now but on the odd occasion I doze off on the couch, I'll find myself waking with a start and fighting to breathe. I still get a bit scared sometimes if I wake on my own in the dark though. I have started sleeping with a little lamp on so that I can see exactly where I am if I do wake up in the night.

"Right babe you ready." Steven's voice snaps me out of my daydream. I turn and see him standing at the kitchen door.

"Yeah, just about. You nervous?" I know he is. As much as he might like to try and hide it, I know he is worried about what I'm going to hear.

"A little but I'll be fine. Let's go before we end up late." I glance at the clock and notice that it is almost one thirty. We have half an hour. Now I know he is nervous, it will only take us two minutes to walk to the

230

office. I say nothing. Grabbing my bag from the kitchen chair, I walk towards him. He takes my hand and we both head out the door.

***

The waiting room is empty. I have never seen it so empty on a Tuesday afternoon. Fiona greets us in her usual cheery manner, but I can see something behind her smile. Of course, she knows what happened to me, I feel like the whole world knows. I want today to go well because I know it will help both of us to talk about everything. According to Fiona, Nate has cleared the rest of his day for us and now I'm the one who is nervous. He obviously thinks we need more than just an hour to air all our problems and I don't know if I am strong enough for the emotional onslaught that awaits. We sit down on the familiar wooden seats that somehow manage to feel alien to me today. Everything seems to have changed. My leg bounces almost involuntarily and Steven reaches over to hold my hand. The bouncing stops.

"Hey are you okay," he whispers.

I can't answer. I don't know what to say. Yes, I'm fine but no I'm not really. I'm starting to realise I'm the more nervous party here. Just as I think I'm going to have to make a run for it, Nate opens his door and calls us in.

"Take a seat guys," Nate says motioning to the new couch in his office. It's green like his old one but not as tattered. I keep focusing on the couch, because if I try to focus on what is ahead, I fear I will have a breakdown.

"So Gina, how are you?"

I nod as I sit next to Steven. "I'm fine Nate."

He raises an eyebrow at me. He keeps his eyes focused on me and I find it very unnerving.

"What? I'm fine honestly."

Steven squeezes my hand and I look up at him. His eyes have the same expression as Nate's. They are both starting to annoy me.

"Would you two stop it I'm fine. For God sake it's like the Spanish Inquisition in here."

"Gina, you have been through some really traumatic events over the last few months. It's natural to want to appear strong and as though you can fight the world but that's the whole point of this session. Tell me how you really feel."

I bow my head. I know I'm fighting a losing battle here. I don't want to appear weak. I don't want them to know that I wake up in the night unable to breathe, feeling like I'm drowning again. I can't tell Steven that I'm scared the ghost of his father will never be gone, that it will haunt me and him forever. Steven softens his grip on my hand and rubs my knuckles. I chance a look at him and his sad expression is my undoing. He is trying his best to stay strong through all this for me, but I know his fears are the same.

"I'm sorry," I whisper.

"In your own time Gina," says Nate.

I hesitate. Where do I start, how do I start? I look at my wrists, unbandaged now but still very raw. "What do you want me to say Nate? That I'm fucking terrified to go to sleep now in case I wake up drowning. That I can't bear to be alone. That I don't want to move in to my new home, the place that was supposed to be my new start, for fear that someone will come and get me. That I'm..."

I look at Steven with tears in my eyes. Taking a huge breath I carry on, I have to. "That I'm scared Steven will never be free of him. I'm scared that every time he looks at me, he will be reminded of what that bastard tried to do to me and what he actually did to him."

I have to look away from Steven to say what I need to next. I can't bear to see the pain in his eyes. "I know what he did Steven. I can't forget what he said, all those awful things he made you do. It makes me sick to my stomach and I'm sorry you never got to confront him. I'm so sorry." I put my head in my hands and sob. Steven pulls me close to him and kisses my hair. Pushing me back slightly he holds my face in his hands, wiping away my tears with his thumbs.

"Gina, I don't care about any of that. I've finally realised that nothing is worth dwelling on. I almost lost the only person I have ever loved and it scared me to death. I could go on for the rest of my life hating a ghost. I can't change anything that happened to me, but I can change the way I view my life and how I live it." His eyes are bright and sincere. "I love you Gina and the fact that you know the most dark, disgusting thing about me and are still sitting here tells me all I need to know about your feelings for me. You will never know how grateful I am that you came in to my life. You saved me."

As I look in to those gorgeous eyes, I'm surprised to see that they don't look pained anymore. I see hope in them, and love.

"So Steven, how do you feel?" Asks Nate. Steven lets go of my face and takes my hand in both of his. He turns his attention to Nate.

"She said she worried about me. You don't worry about someone you don't love."

Nate nods his head. "Did you ever doubt that she loved you?"

"I knew when he had her alone, he would tell her about what happened to me as a child. I knew he was going to try and ruin my life and having Gina be disgusted by me was his way of doing that. He could have robbed me of every penny I have but if he turned her against me, I would be worth nothing."

Steven turns back to me and I feel as though some of the fog has lifted. The future looks brighter for us. I'm not naive, I realise that just saying things out loud won't magically fix everything but it's a start. It means we each know that we don't need to keep everything bottled up inside. We know so much about each other now and we have been given a second chance to do things right.

He leans in and kisses me and it's a 'you and me against the world' kind of kiss. We don't need any words, although Nate's clearing of his throat tells us he hasn't quite finished with us. We look at each other and laugh.

***

Nate was right to clear his schedule because it is almost three hours later when we finally emerge from his office.

"Do you want to go out for dinner?" Steven asks.

"Sounds good to me. Where do you want to go?"

"Let's go to Black. It's Indian tonight and I fancy curry and a beer."

The first and last time I was at Black was when all this mess really started to take over our lives. It seems like so long ago and so much has happened since then.

I never really got to enjoy it properly, so a nice quiet dinner together sounds lovely.

"Yeah that's a plan. Can I go and get changed though? I look like I've been dragged through a hedge backwards."

I'm startled when he grabs my waist and spins me in to him. He holds me so close I can feel his heart beating. "You are beautiful no matter what Gina Harper." His beautiful blue eyes are striking and I melt in to him.

This is where I belong. This, in his arms no matter where we may be, is home. I love this man more than I ever realised I could and I know if we can get through what has happened over the last few months, we can conquer anything life has to throw at us.

CHAPTER 29

STANDING IN THE ENTRANCE hallway of what should be my new home, my new beginning, the only feeling I have is fear. I shouldn't feel like this. This is not how I saw things going. I don't even want to venture into the apartment. This is the first time I have even been here since it officially became mine.

It's hard to believe that less than two weeks ago I was excited to have signed all my paperwork so that the place was finally mine. Little over half an hour later events were set in motion that would lead to me standing here feeling like a frightened child. I don't understand why though. Colin is dead, he can't hurt me or Steven anymore, we are safe. So why am I still constantly looking over my shoulder?

Ever since I left the hospital, I haven't been on my own and today is no exception. Charlie has come to stay for the weekend because Mark is away to a conference at London Zoo. She doesn't want to be left alone. She is only three weeks away from her due date and is terrified of going into labour alone.

"Gina this apartment is bloody beautiful."

"It is but I can't stay here on my own Charlie."

She walks across the hallway towards me. I expect her to say something sarcastic or snarky, but she surprises me by pulling me into a hug.

"Oh honey I know this has all been terrible but you're stronger than this. You survived an abduction, a car crash and a drowning for God sake."

I shake my head as she lets me go. "I know but it's not over and probably won't be for a long time. The police have told us that there will be a Fatal Accident Inquiry into the accident because it involved a sudden death." The thought of having to constantly re-live my ordeal fills me with dread. "That could take up to two years to even happen."

"Oh, honey I'm so sorry but I'm so glad you're still here. I only just got you back."

I smile at her. I know terrible she feels that I was taken 'on her watch'.

We walk through to the open plan living room and kitchen. The window at the kitchen looks out on to the courtyard of The Italian Centre and the one on the opposite end in the living room has views down on to

Ingram Street.

She's right, this place is stunning. I had high hopes of living here right inside the beating heart of the city. The nightlife in The Merchant City area is fantastic and the shopping on my doorstep is perfect but it all just seems like a waste now.

I almost jump out of my skin when Charlie's phone starts blaring *'Funky Town'*.

"Oh it's Nikki. Sorry Gina I need to take this, something must be wrong she never phones me." She answers the phone and walks, more like waddles, off in the direction of one of the bedrooms.

I make my way to the gleaming kitchen sink and absentmindedly turn the tap on and off, on and off, and on and off. I can feel my eyes start to glaze over but am quickly brought back to earth with a bang when I hear Charlie scream, it echoes in the empty apartment. I run in the direction of the noise and find Charlie in the master bedroom, still on the phone. She turns to look at me and throws me an apologetic look. *'Sorry'* she mouths.

"What did mum and dad say when you told them? And they were okay with it? Oh my God Nikki I'm so excited. Email me with your plans and I'll do what I can from this end. Oh sis you have no idea how happy you've made me. Okay, speak soon. Love you too honey."

As she hangs up the phone, I realise from the huge smile on her face that it was good news.

"Charlie you almost gave me a heart attack. What the hell has happened?"

She looks at me a little sheepishly but can't hold it long enough for effect as the smile spreads over her face again. "Nikki is moving to Scotland. Can you believe it Gina? She's coming here to stay. Forever." She has tears in her eyes. I am genuinely happy for her. I know she misses her family.

"That's really amazing news Charlie, when is she coming?"

"She won't be here until the end of February but when she gets here, she's not going back. Oh Gina you have no idea how happy this has made me. But that's not even all of it. My dad has finally decided to retire at the end of the year. My parents are coming back to the UK with her too. Dad passed his official retirement age two years ago, but he loved his job so much he decided not to go when he should have."

"Are they coming to Scotland too?"

"No, they are moving to London. When I said my dad was retiring, what I should have said was that he is retiring from his post at The British High Commission in South Africa and coming back here to work at the Foreign Office. Mum's not happy that he isn't giving up completely but she's at least getting to come home. She would rather be back in Glasgow, but she doesn't think dad will stay in the job much longer, so she might get her wish."

I'm feeling a lot better now that her happiness has lifted the mood.

"Fancy a wee celebration dinner honey?" I smile at her.

"Do I ever? I really want a bloody, mooing steak but I'm not supposed to eat rare meat."

"Yeah and since when did Charlie ever do as she was told?"

She throws her head back and laughs.

"Right steak it is then and don't tell anyone."

"I promise, it's our secret."

I'm so glad to be getting out of here; the whole place is making me feel lousy.

***

The Grill Room at 29 on Royal Exchange Square is a beautiful place to eat. It has great views down onto the square and the Modern Art Gallery. Thankfully we are seated at a window. We both love a bit of people watching.

"So what is Nikki going to do when she gets here?" I ask when our drink order has been taken.

"She's been working at a software development company in Pretoria, but I think by the sound of things she isn't progressing anywhere in the job. She moved to a different department, but it still wasn't enough for her. She's a clever girl you know. The last time I went to visit she was working on some app that was going to revolutionise the world according to her."

"What happened with it?"

"She tried to get grant funding and support from her employer, but everything was denied. She said to me a while ago that she was fed up with her life. She's only twenty-six, how can you be fed up at that age?"

We sit chatting and eating for the next hour and a half, mostly about Charlie's sister. She's so excited that her family is coming, it's just the news she needed. After everything she has told me about Nikki, I really can't wait to meet her. I shook her hand and said a brief hello to her once when we were at Uni, but she would only have been about fifteen then.

As we leave the square and walk into Queen Street to hail a taxi, Charlie grabs my hand and we both stop.

"What's up honey?" I ask as I look at the tears forming in her eyes.

"I don't even know why I'm crying here Gina, must be the hormones. This question I have to ask you is a bloody foregone conclusion, but I want to do it right." She hesitates for a few seconds then composes herself enough to speak. "I know there's no date set yet, but will you be my chief bridesmaid at my wedding?" She smiles as a few tears fall from her eyes.

"Oh Charlie of course I will. Hey, don't be so upset you'll set me off. We both know I can cry for Scotland given half the chance. And I would have thought it was a given anyway. If you hadn't asked me, I would have been well pissed." I smile at her and nudge her shoulder with mine.

She laughs and swipes her tears away. "I'm sorry babe, this is happening too often these days. Who knew I'd ever be an emotional wreck?"

"Well honey in the last year I have seen just about everything, but you being an emotional wreck wasn't one I thought I'd encounter."

Charlie nudges me with her elbow. "Come on let's get home. I'm dying to get into some comfy pj's and put my poor swollen feet up."

We laugh as we get into the taxi.

***

The sound of the piano and singing wafts down the stairs as Charlie and I enter Steven's building. She looks at me with a puzzled expression.

"Where is that coming from? Are there speakers out here too?" She asks.

I laugh. "Steven must be having a little go on the piano."

"That's Steven? He's really good."

I nod my agreement and we make our way into the apartment. The music hits us full force as we walk through the front door and the sight that greets us makes me go weak in the knees.

Steven is sitting at the piano dressed only in a pair of pyjama trousers, his fingers moving effortlessly across the keys and his back muscles rippling with every tiny movement he makes.

I'm finding it hard to concentrate on standing upright but when I look at Charlie I burst into hysterics. Her jaw is almost on the floor and she can't take her eyes off him. I nudge her with my elbow. "Hey you, eyes off."

"Well it's there on show Gina, sorry but that view is fair game."

Steven hears us and immediately stops playing, turning on the stool and flashing that knicker-ripping smile.

"Hi ladies," he says as he gets up and strides over to us, pulling me into a long and deep kiss.

"Ugh thanks for wasting my wee fantasy there guys. I'm going to get out of these shoes, my damn feet are like balloons."

Charlie saunters up the stairs to her room as Mr. Hotbod leads me into the kitchen. As soon as we are through the doors to the kitchen, he spins me round and lifts me onto a bar stool. Standing between my legs he puts his hands in to my hair and pulls me to him. The kiss is slow and sensual and I'm lost in him. I run my hands over his perfectly toned shoulders, feeling the muscles moving beneath my fingers. He releases my lips but keeps his face close to mine.

"Hmm to what do I owe the pleasure?" I whisper.

"Just for being you. I love you Gina."

"Right that's it." The voice from behind us booms. "We are having none of that while I'm here. If I aint getting any, neither are you. And don't even think about doing it while I'm sleeping, I'll know," Charlie says, wagging her finger at us with a big smile on her face. She has changed into pyjamas and a big fluffy fleece housecoat, the belt barely tied round her huge bump.

"Sorry Charlie, do you both want a hot chocolate? I have mini marshmallows and cream," says Steven winking at her.

"Steven you're a bloody charmer. You don't need to seduce me with your sexy wink, you said the word chocolate. I'm all yours," she laughs at him and takes a seat beside me at the breakfast bar.

We both watch Steven for a few moments. I'm seriously in lust with this guy. He really is a stunning specimen of maleness, and he knows exactly what he is doing to me. Every so often he flexes his back muscles and it is causing stirrings in me that I really don't appreciate when I'm sitting next to my very pregnant friend in her huge polka dot housecoat. I take in his sculpted shoulders and the way his lean muscles direct your eyes down to the little dimples at the base of his back.

Remembering myself I turn to Charlie. She is not looking at Steven anymore. She has her eyes closed and is rubbing her back with both hands.

"You okay honey?" I ask and Steven turns around, a worried expression on his face.

"Oh, it's nothing really. These Braxton Hicks are getting quite painful. It's making me even more nervous about what's to come."

"Both of you go through to the TV room and I'll bring these to you when they are ready. I got Gerry to get a few films for you to watch."

Charlie gives him a thankful smile and we make our way through the apartment. Charlie sits down on the couch and puts her feet up and I take a look at the DVD's.

"Let's see if Gerry's female side was showing when he bought these."

"DVD's? Old school, I like it," says Charlie laughing. God we are getting old when we think DVD's are old school.

The first is Grease.

"Hmm…yeah, I like that one but I'm not really in

the mood to watch a sing along. What's next?" Charlie says.

"Dirty Dancing. That's a contender." I hold up the box and we both nod.

"Oh yeah," says Charlie as I place it on the table in front of us.

"We also have Pretty Woman, The Breakfast Club, The First Wives Club and ... oh God no Gerry," I laugh.

"What?" Says Charlie trying to see the title of the last DVD. She grabs it out of my hand.

"Fucking Knocked Up? Is he trying to scare the shit out of me?"

"Let's watch it," I say laughing and am rewarded with a pillow to the face.

"Oh my God is this really what girls get up to on sleepovers?" Says Steven from behind us. Charlie and I look at each other and burst into hysterics.

"Chandler," we say in unison.

"Here you go girls." He places a tray down on the table with two hot chocolates with cream and marshmallows and a huge bowl of popcorn.

"So, what are you going to watch?"

"Don't know but certainly not this," says Charlie holding up the Knocked Up DVD.

Steven laughs. "Well I'm away to do some paperwork. I'll see you in bed later babe," he says as he leans down and kisses me on the head. Then he surprises both of us as he leans over to Charlie and whispers to her, "I chose that one."

As soon as he has said it, he makes a run for the door as Charlie fires the DVD case at him.

"Bitch," she shouts as it hits the floor and the DVD skids across the room.

CHAPTER 30

THE MORE I LOOK at this awesome man lying sleeping beside me, the more I think I fall in love with him. Steven is lying on his back and I know that beneath the sheet lying across his hips he is naked. He has one arm up on the pillow above his head and the other is on his chest. He looks so peaceful. Ever since he realised that his father is no longer a threat to him, to us, he has slept right through the night beside me. It was as though his body had been holding a breath for the last twenty years and finally it was able to release it. This poor man has never really lived because of the terror he endured as a child and the anger he had as an adult. I watch his chest rise and fall and match my breathing to his.

Reaching over, I touch his perfectly formed, most kissable lips and his eyes flutter open. I'm rewarded with a smile and the sleepy blinking of those beautiful eyes.

"Morning handsome," I whisper and place a soft kiss on his lips.

"Mmm. Morning gorgeous," he responds and startles me when he pulls me over on top of him.

"Oh yes good morning indeed." I smile when I feel his hardness against my bum cheek.

"Doesn't take much with you babe."

"You do know you don't need to flatter me don't you? You are on to a sure thing here."

Steven reaches up and strokes my cheek, his features softening. "I love you beautiful girl. You have no idea how happy it makes me to wake up with you every morning. I want to ask you something."

I'm intrigued. "Fire away."

"Will you wake up with me every morning?"

My brows knit into a frown. "I already do wake up with you every morning. Well I do now."

He smiles and I realise I have got it all wrong, yet again.

"No, I want to wake up with you every morning forever. Move in with me Gina, I don't want to let you go."

Talk about being blindsided. "But what about my flat? I've only just signed the missives. God the money only left my bank account last week."

"Keep it. You bought it outright, yes?"

I nod.

"Well it's yours to do what you want with. Rent it out, it's in a prime location and it'll make you money."

I think about it for a second. I know it makes sense but at the same time I'm scared. When I went to see the place yesterday, it felt tainted somehow. I didn't get any sense of it being home. I think a lot of my anxiety actually stems from not wanting to be on my own anymore. I have kind of slotted myself in to this little thing Steven and I have going and it is nice being here with him. I'm already living with him in some capacity anyway. He is also right about the flat generating an income since I am effectively unemployed and what I do have will not last forever. I watch him as he reads my face.

"I don't expect it to be a decision you make right now. Think about it. I can see it's troubling you. But know this, I will make it worth your while." A flex of his cock at my back accompanies his cheeky grin.

I laugh wryly. "Oh good God you perv. I was about to give you an answer but now I'm going to make you wait."

He holds up his hands in surrender. "Okay, I won't touch you. Tell me, what's your answer?"

"Nope not telling you."

He takes me by surprise when he flips me onto my

back and looms over me. "Are you going to tell me now?"

"Nope."

Steven grabs my wrists and pulls my hands above my head, holding them in place with one hand. He holds the other above me in a claw shape. "Will you tell me now?"

I know what is going to happen if I say no this time, but I can't help myself.

"No," I giggle and no sooner has the word left my lips than I'm being tickled to within an inch of my life. I'm completely naked which gives him access to my bare skin making the sensation even more pronounced.

"Please stop." I can't stop laughing. I bloody hate getting tickled. My dad once tickled me so hard when I was a little girl, I peed myself from laughing. I have always been worried about doing it again. It wouldn't be very ladylike if I were to pee the bed right now.

"Tell me or I'll keep tickling."

I can't take it anymore, I hate letting him win.

"Okay, okay I'll tell you but on one condition."

"Which is?"

I pull my hands free and wrap my arms round his neck, pulling myself up.

"Fuck me first," I whisper.

He smiles. He knows what my answer is going to be, but he obliges anyway. He trails butterfly kisses down my neck, over my collarbone and his lips lightly skim my nipples as his mouth trails ever lower. I can feel the intense heat pooling in my belly. His moves are so soft and slow and yet my body feels ready to explode under him. I gasp as his head disappears and he runs his tongue over me in a long, slow sweep. My body responds of its own accord, shamelessly writhing beneath him. His tongue presses harder and I can't help it. I grab his head and pull him in to me. He takes the hint and pushes his tongue inside me as far as he can, his nose hitting my clit in just the right way and I give in and let the orgasm take me. My hips won't stop moving, grinding into his face. It's so fucking hot and I come again and again as he refuses to give up.

When I think my body has floated away and left me, he rears up over me and before I can register what he is doing he pushes in to me, going as deep as he can as fast as he can. It takes me by surprise. His movements are fast and hard and I can't help but watch what he is doing. This is only serving to make another orgasm bubble up. He moves faster and faster until I'm almost shunted up the bed and as I come in great waves, I feel his rhythm stutter and I know he is close. When his own release takes him, he collapses on top of me. My hips won't stop gyrating though and I bask in the glow of another little mini orgasm.

"So, I have done as you asked, now, what's your

answer?"

I look into his beautiful eyes, which have looked so much more vibrant lately. They aren't quite pleading but there is a longing. I need to put him out of his misery.

"Yes, I will move in with you and I have an idea already who I can let my flat to."

Steven's face lights up and he grabs my face and kisses me long and hard. "I don't give a fuck about the flat right now. Do you realise how happy you've just made me?"

"I don't think I need to guess."

He pulls me right in beside him and we spoon until we doze off to sleep again.

***

I watch Charlie as she sits at the table in the kitchen. She doesn't really look too great this morning and I'm a little worried about her.

"Are you okay honey?" I ask as I sit down opposite her, handing her a mug of tea.

"Oh babe I'm just sore. I can't get comfortable at night right now and I constantly have to get up to pee. I'm telling you these last three weeks are going to be the longest of my life." She sits back and runs her hands over her belly.

"How do you fancy going for a wee spa treatment

today. There's a place right down on Royal Terrace next to Steven's office. It might help relax you."

"Sounds good to me," Charlie says and holds up her mug, clinking it on mine.

"Right girls I'm off," Steven says walking in to the kitchen while hauling a jumper over his head.

"You do realise you're going to get your arse handed to you today don't you? My dad is brilliant at golf."

He laughs and walks over to me. He puts his hand in my hair and tips my head back, kissing me seductively. I can hear Charlie making fake sick noises beside us. "Thanks for the vote of confidence. You know now that we are living together you should be a bit nicer to me."

"Excuse me?" I look at Charlie's questioning expression.

"Oh yeah sorry," I say to Charlie but give Steven an 'I'll deal with you later' look as he slinks his way out the door laughing.

"Spill bitch," says Charlie as soon as we hear the front door close.

"Well Steven asked me to move in with him this morning, so I said yes."

"Oh my God Gina, this is big news. I'm so happy for you but what about your flat, you've only just bought it?"

"Well that's something I was going to run past you."

"Okay, this sounds interesting."

"Where is Nikki staying when she gets here?" Charlie's smile is huge when I mention her little sister.

"She's moving to Glasgow, she says Edinburgh is too posh for her. Would you consider renting your flat to her?"

"That's exactly what I want to do. Does she have a job lined up or interviews or anything?"

"Yes her boss has put her in touch with a company based over in the city centre, so she has an interview with them next month. Gina this is so cool. I'll need to make sure mum and dad give you her rent money until she can pay it herself." Poor Charlie has tears in her eyes.

"She can stay rent free until she gets settled. As soon as she gets a salary she can start paying, obviously she'll get mates rates though."

And that does it, she is in floods of tears and I'm thanked over and over again through tears and sniffs.

**

Charlie and I decide against the Spa and are now sitting in the beautiful Willow Tearooms in the city centre having afternoon tea. This tearoom is on Buchanan Street and is very Charles Rennie Mackintosh, a design synonymous with Glasgow.

"Wait till you hear what my midwife said to me," says Charlie with a mouthful of cucumber sandwich. "She was talking about what happens after the baby is born. So, she was going through things like breastfeeding, where baby will sleep, what nappies I'll use, you know stuff like that. Then she started talking about sex. I tried to be funny and said, 'oh well that's what got me in to this state in the first place' and she totally stared me down. She said it was a serious matter and told me to behave. I felt like a kid at school."

I laugh at her. Her sense of humour is amazing and I can just imagine the midwife's face. "So what did she say about sex then?"

"We can't do it for at least six weeks after the baby is born. I'm going to be like a born-again virgin by then. Poor Mark is going to be best friends with his hand."

We are greeted by tuts from two older ladies in tweed suits sitting at the table beside us. Charlie just laughs.

"That's not all, she started talking about birth control. I think the cheeky bitch thought I would end up pregnant again straight away. I don't know what to do about that though. The pill I was on didn't really agree with me, as you can see. What one are you on?"

The cold feeling of dread that falls over me in that

moment makes me feel sick.

"Gina are you alright? I swear to God I actually saw the colour drain out of your face."

"Sorry Charlie," I manage to splutter as I run to the toilet, nearly knocking over a waitress in the process. As soon as I'm in the cubicle I slide down on my knees and proceed to throw up my afternoon tea. As I sit with my head in my hands, I hear Charlie come in.

"Gina what's happened, you're scaring me."

I get up on very shaky legs and open the door. As soon as I see her, I burst into tears.

"Hey, tell me what's wrong," she says softly.

"Oh Charlie, I've messed up. Majorly messed up."

"On what?"

"I forgot all about my pill."

Her eyes widen. "How many have you missed? If it's only one it will be alright as long as you take it straight away won't it?"

"The last one I took was the day before we went out in Edinburgh."

Charlie's expression is one of pure shock. "Oh fuck Gina, two weeks!"

I shake my head in disbelief. "How could I have been so stupid Charlie?"

"Hey honey this isn't your fault. Don't beat yourself up. Come on let's get out of here." Charlie takes my hand and we leave the tearoom with my head swimming in all different directions, wondering what I'm going to do.

CHAPTER 31

THE QUEUE IN BOOTS pharmacy is huge and is moving at a snail's pace. Charlie is holding a box with two pregnancy tests in it. I actually can't believe this is real. We both stand in silence as we edge closer to the till. When it is our turn to get served, we end up at the till of an older lady, possibly in her sixties with a tight grey perm and glasses on a gold neck chain. Charlie hands her the box and as she scans it, she looks at us, at Charlie in particular, eyeing her bump and giving an accusatory look.

I pay for the test and we head out of the shop arm in arm. Charlie walks so fast she is almost dragging me out the door.

"Christ Charlie slow down."

She comes to a halt shaking her head. "That fucking bitch was giving me the evil eye in there, did you see her? I wanted to knock her right out."

God she's a badass today. "Charlie are you okay?"

"Yeah I just feel... I don't even know Gina. I'm so agitated today."

"And I've done nothing to help with that have I?"

Charlie wraps her arm around my shoulder. "Gina, I'm here for you every step of the way honey. If you are pregnant it's not the worst thing in the world is it?"

"It wouldn't be under normal circumstances, but this has just been typical of mine and Steven's relationship from the very start. I'm fucking fed up with it Charlie."

She takes my arm and hails a taxi. As soon as we are settled in the back, I put my head on her shoulder and stare off into space. When did my life become a bloody soap opera?

***

When we are back at the apartment Charlie hands me the bag with the pregnancy tests in it.

"Charlie I can't do this yet."

She takes my hand. "It's okay honey. Do you want a coffee?"

"Yeah that sounds good. Throw a fucking whisky in it as well."

Charlie smiles at me but it doesn't reach her eyes. She feels sorry for me. I just feel pathetic. She's right,

261

there are worse things than a baby. I was kidnapped and almost died so I guess this is a way of the universe making me realise I'm still alive. Charlie brings the mugs to the table and sits down opposite me.

"Oh Gina, I'm goddamn exhausted."

"Yeah and I've only gone and added to your stress."

She is about to reply when her phone rings. "Sorry honey it's Mark, I need to take this."

Charlie gets up and leaves the room and I'm left with my thoughts. I suppose it's now or never really. The sooner I know the sooner I can make plans. I grab the box from the table and head into the cloakroom toilet. Fumbling with the bag I tip the box out on to the countertop. This is not something I ever thought I'd be doing two months into a relationship.

I think about Charlie and instantly feel bad for the way I have acted in front of her. She and Mark were only dating a couple of months when she fell pregnant.

Unwrapping the box, I slide out one of the tests. God there's so much packaging. I pull open the plastic wrapper and the little stick falls out. The good thing is I do need to pee. I sit down on the toilet and hold the stick under the stream. A tear falls silently from my eye and lands on my bare leg. I stand, fix my clothes and place the test face down. This is going to be the longest four minutes of my life.

I can't turn the white stick over and I still can't look at it lying there next to the sink. I'm utterly terrified. What will I do if it is positive? What will Steven do? Will he leave me? Will he hate me? Will he think I have done this on purpose? I feel hot tears burn behind my eyes. Oh God this cannot be happening to me. Not now. Not after everything we've been through.

There's a slight knock at the bathroom door. "Gina are you okay?" Says Charlie, her voice soft and calm. I open the door and walk out.

"Charlie I can't do this. I can't look at it. Maybe if I don't know it will just go away." I head past her and out the bathroom door.

When I'm in the kitchen, I take a bottle of wine from the fridge and pour a glass. My hands are shaking so much I'm surprised I'm even able to hold the bottle steady enough to pour it.

"Gina you need to put that down."

Charlie's voice is shaky behind me. She is standing in the doorway holding the pregnancy test down by her side with a look of shock on her face.

Any sense of composure I think I have goes in that moment and, as the wine glass slips from my hand and smashes to pieces on the floor, I feel the colour drain from my face. "Oh God Charlie no."

Thanks for reading

Gina and Steven's journey
continues in Heart and Soul

Read on for a sneak peek of Heart
and Soul,
Book 3 in the Soul Series

Keep up to date with news and
upcoming book releases by visiting:
www.clstewart.co.uk

Sign up for exclusive content and
offers

HEART AND SOUL

CHAPTER 1

HOSPITAL WAITING ROOMS ARE sometimes pretty depressing places. This one is no different. It doesn't matter that the walls are filled with posters of cute little babies and smiling mothers. The whole place is making me feel sick. As I stand next to the water cooler holding the flimsy plastic cup in my hand, a very heavily pregnant woman and her partner come in. They take a seat and I watch them for a few seconds. She rubs her belly and he rubs her back and talks soothingly to her. He tells her he loves her and he is so proud of her. They look so happy.

Tears fall silently from my eyes and I turn and face the window. It's dark outside and I can see my reflection in the glass. I look like shit. Turning to the side I look at my body's profile. I don't look any different and I don't feel any different. I would have thought I would have known if I was pregnant without having to do a test. Charlie told me all about how she realised she was pregnant. The sore boobs, throwing up, missed periods and such. I have had none of those.

As it happens, I still don't even know. I didn't get a chance to look at the test and neither did Charlie. Right now, I'm in one of the waiting rooms of the Princess Royal Maternity unit while my friend is getting checked over by a midwife. This hospital is becoming far too familiar to me these days. Baby Georgie's timing is impeccable and she's not even here yet. Charlie is in labour and, according to the midwife, probably has been since yesterday.

I finish my cup of water and head outside to call Mark again. I've been unable to get hold of him since before we left Steven's apartment. Bugger it! Steven. I haven't called him. As soon as my phone comes to life it rings in my hand. It's Mark.

"Mark. Thank God."

"Shit Gina I've been trying to call for the last fifteen minutes since I got your message. I'm freaking out here. What's happened? Is Charlie okay?"

"Mark..."

"I'm trying to get a flight organised but it's such short notice..."

"Mark..."

"...I've explained to my colleagues that I need to..."

Good God it's like talking to my mother, I can't get a word in. "MARK!" I shout and he stops talking.

"Shit, I'm sorry Gina I'm panicking."

"I know. First of all, calm down. Charlie is at the Princess Royal Maternity and she is being checked over right now. I don't know how advanced things are, but she is in labour. I think she had just got off the phone to you and her waters broke in Steven's bathroom. I'm just about to phone Steven so I'll see if there is something he can do for you okay. I'll call you back."

I can hear his sigh of relief that he now knows Charlie is okay. "Thanks Gina, I'll keep the line open."

"Right stay where you are and I'll call you back." We hang up and I call Steven. He answers on the second ring.

"Hey gorgeous I was just thinking about you."

"Hey listen, Charlie's waters broke this afternoon, she's in labour. We are at the hospital now."

"Jesus Gina you should have called me earlier."

I feel so bad that he was an afterthought, but things were quite frantic. "I've only just managed to get a hold of Mark. He's still in London, he's having trouble getting a flight quick enough."

"Leave that with me. I'll deal with it, I have his number. You go and be with Charlie, is there anything she needs?"

271

"I think she really could do with having her hospital bag here but it's at her flat. She obviously wasn't expecting to need it this weekend."

"I'll get Gerry to pick it up and I'll be there as soon as I can okay."

He's such a good soul and seems quite calm while I have an internal crisis.

"Thanks Steven I really appreciate this."

"Anything for you babe you know that. I need to go and sort Mark out. Get back to Charlie. Love you Gina."

"Love you too Steven." I say as we hang up and the breath I take comes out stuttered. I give myself a shake, I can't dwell on my own problems right now, my friend needs me.

Charlie is sitting up in bed reading a magazine when I get back to the ward.

"How did your examination go darling?"

"Well I'm five centimetres and the contractions are coming along nicely apparently. I'm now in active labour. Gina you should try some of this stuff. It's amazeballs. Ha." Charlie's expression looks strange and she holds up a hose with a mouthpiece attached to it.

"What is it?"

"Gas and air. Best thing invented, I want to take it home." She laughs then abruptly throws her head back, her contraction quickly turning the laugh to a pained growl. "Gina this is going to kill me."

"What about all the drugs you were going to have?"

"Fuck no, I've heard all these horror stories so I'm going without. Did you get a hold of Mark?"

"Yeah honey but he's having trouble getting out of London. Steven is going to help. Don't know what he will be able to do but he said he'll handle it. He is also getting Gerry to get your bag from your house."

Her smile is thankful. "Gina I really need him here."

I can see she is getting distressed about this. "I'm here for as long as you need me honey okay."

"Thanks Gina."

My phone pings with a text and I quickly pull it out of my pocket and turn it to silent before I get told off. "Oops. It's from Steven." I read it and smile at Charlie. "He says he got Mark a flight on a wee private plane doing an empty return journey to Glasgow. I have no idea what that means but he says the flight should get into Glasgow in about an hour."

"Thank God. Hear that Georgie?" Charlie says patting her belly. "Your daddy won't be long so you just stay in there as long as you can okay baby girl."

"Can I get you anything honey? Do you want a drink?"

"No I'm fine babe I've got some here. Why don't we

talk about the elephant in the room right now? And I don't mean me."

I don't think I can talk about this now. I'm having a hard time as it is, being surrounded by all these pregnant women and babies.

"Let's not."

"You're going to have to talk about it Gina. I can see it's eating you up."

Of course she is right. On one hand I know I have always wanted children but on the other it is way too soon. Steven and I have been through so much in the last few months we haven't had enough time alone to really get to know each other. I also don't know what his reaction will be. I don't even know if he wants kids.

"Oh Charlie what am I going to do if that test is positive? What did you do with it anyway?"

"It's still on the worktop in Steven's kitchen. If it's positive you will just have to get on with it and Steven will too. Listen you do know you are going to have to talk to him about this regardless of how it turns out. God Gina these are getting painful."

Charlie grabs my hand and squeezes it tight. Her face contorts and she goes through her breathing exercises. I feel like a dab hand at this now. When she is done, she carries on talking as if nothing happened and we sit chatting and breathing through the contractions for the next hour.

***

The midwife joins us and as I stand to leave Charlie's room the door opens.

Mark has finally arrived and he rushes at Charlie with tears in his eyes. "Oh my God Charlie I'm so sorry. I got here as fast as I could." He says to her, kissing her hand. He turns to me.

"Gina I can't thank you enough. You and Steven are the best. He got me a flight on a private plane and he picked me up from the airport himself too."

"Is he here?"

"Yeah he's parking the car. I was out before he had even stopped." Mark turns back to Charlie who is having another contraction. The midwife makes her comfortable and I give Mark's shoulder a squeeze.

"Right you two I'm going to find Steven. Good luck honey." I say to Charlie and kiss her head.

"Thanks Gina." She smiles at me and I blow her a kiss as I leave. As soon as I'm out the door, the rush of emotion coursing through me takes my legs out from under me and I collapse in a heap by the door. The next voice I hear pulls me out of the darkness as I'm lifted into Steven's arms.

CHAPTER 2

"GINA." STEVEN STANDS ME upright and takes my hand. "Come with me."

I'm led away from Charlie's room and down the hallway. Steven pushes open the waiting room door and thankfully it is empty. He closes the door behind us and stands with his hand on the door for a few seconds as I sit down on a seat at the window.

"It's been a bit of a day for you today hasn't it?"

I nod and look into his eyes. Something is wrong. He stays silent for a few moments though it feels like hours. When he eventually speaks, he doesn't look at me.

"Do you have something you need to tell me Gina?"

Fuck!

He puts his hand in his pocket and pulls out the

pregnancy test. I think I'm about to faint.

"Steven I'm so sorry."

He is holding it so that I can't see the result on it, but he can. "Why are you sorry? Is this yours?"

I can't actually tell if he is angry or not and it is throwing me a little.

"Yes, it is but I don't know what the result is." I bow my head. This is the worst thing that could have happened to me today and I fear that either way this result is going to change things between us.

"Do you want to know what the result is?"

"Not really."

"Why?"

Because I don't want you to leave me. Because I don't want you to hate me. Because I love you. I know what I want to say but the words won't come out. I shrug my shoulders instead. I feel like a child who has been caught lying.

"Gina look at me."

I do, slowly and see the pained expression on his face.

"God Steven. What does it say?"

"Before I show you, I want you to know something. I love you Gina and no matter what, I will always be here. I told you I was never letting you go, and I meant it."

I put my head in my hands. "I'm so sorry, this isn't

how things were supposed to be."

"Gina, look."

I lift my head and look at the test. There, in the little window is……………

To Be Continued

Printed in Great Britain
by Amazon